Dangerous Thirst 2

Shattered Taste

By

Ja'Lisa Marie

Published in the United States by Ja'Lisa Marie

Copyright © 2022 by Ja'Lisa Marie.

ISBN: 979-8-9861560-1-9

First printing edition 2022.

Library of Congress Control Number:

Dangerous Thirst 2, Shattered Taste is a work of fiction. It is not meant to depict, portray, or represent any particular real persons. All the characters, incidents, and dialogues are a product of the author's imagination and are not to be construed as real. Any references or similarities to actual or historical events, entities, real people, living or dead, or real locales are used fictitiously and are intended to give the novel a sense of reality. Any similarity in other names, characters, entities, places, and incidents is entirely coincidental.

Cover Layout & Design: Jay Covers

Printed in the United States of America

Email: jalisamarie.ink@gmail.com
FB: www.facebook.com/authorjalisa.marie.3
IG: www.instagram.com/authoressjalisa

Dedication

In Loving Memory of my Little brother Miguel "Mygzz" Santana.
Race In Peace Yota!

I Love and Miss You, Kid!

Table of Contents

INTRODUCTION

$\mathcal{T}$he cathedral church's doors closed as the Master of Ceremonies instructed all the guests to stand to their feet. They all brewed with excitement. It was the moment they had all been waiting for. As the doors began to open back up slowly, the piano's sounds, followed by Jennifer Hudson's song *Giving Myself* filled the air in a loud yet subtle tone.

After a few short seconds of waiting, Royelle gracefully walked out with Rayford to her right and Adala to her left. She could see some guests smiling and some with tears falling down their cheeks, but her main focus was standing at the altar. She couldn't believe that this was the moment her life would completely change. She was going from Ms. Blevins to Mrs. Kingsley in a blink of an eye.

Her White and Gold lace mermaid dress with the sweetheart cut and chapel length train was as sophisticated as everyone assumed it would be. She wowed every guest who laid eyes on her. Her hair was pulled up into a high polished ponytail with big soft pin curls, accompanied by a V-shaped Crystal Queen Tiara that fell just between her perfectly arched eyebrows, and her makeup was impalpable.

The raindrop earrings she wore matched her bracelet, and her White shoes with the Gold heels complimented her dress flawlessly. Her beautiful cascade

1

bouquet was eleven inches wide, twenty-one inches long, made with Gold sprayed open roses and rosebuds, purple mini roses, greenery, and fillers. The thick padded handle was wrapped in gold satin, decorated with royal purple organza bows and ribbons. She looked like something out of a fairytale. No one could refute that she took her time finding the right everything for her day.

"You may all be seated," The officiant said as Royelle made her final stop to the altar. "Who gives this woman to this man?" He asked.

"We Do," Rayford and Adala said in sync.

Each of them hugged Royelle before taking their seat, giving Trevion the floor to stand next to his fiancé. The cameras were flashing, and the whispers of how tasteful and dignified everyone looked were flowing throughout the function room. Royelle and Trevion heard none of it as they gazed deeply into each other.

Trevion could not stop smiling at the beauty before him. He had seen Royelle on her great days and some of her worse, but he had never seen her as stunning as she was at that very moment. Every detail she put into the wedding was worth every minute and dime they put into it.

After some quick words of encouragement and the traditional vow promises, the officiant requested to have the rings presented. Xandra took Royelle's bouquet and passed her Trevion's band, and Raymelle passed Trevion Royelle's two and a half-carat White Gold Emerald-cut ring. It shined so brightly that people in the street could probably see the iridescent rays coming from it.

The officiant started to give instructions as they placed the rings on one another. First, Royelle to Trevion and then Trevion to Royelle. When she looked down at the ring, she quickly looked back up and smiled at him as he put it on her finger. She was shocked to see it wasn't the one she had initially picked out; it was much better. "Thank you." She whispered. He winked his eye at her, and they both faced the officiant for some final words.

"And now the moment you all have been waiting for. I now pronounce you husband and wife!" The officiant shouted. "You may now kiss your bride!"

Trevion reached into Royelle's space, pulled her veil up behind her

2

head, and began to exchange a passionate potion kiss with her. It was so deep and loving that the guest got goosebumps just from watching.

"Ok, bums! That's enough!" Yelled Xandra. "Let's get this party started!"

As Royelle started to respond, a dark black cloud covered her eyes. Everything went pitch black. The day that started out so beautiful and serene, filled with peace and love, had just reduced itself to stark darkness filled with nothing. The joys of the bright sunlight gazing through the crystal-painted windows, the soft sounds of instruments, and the aroma from the columns of bouquets that filled the sanctuary were no more. Everything changed in an instant.

CHAPTER 1:
BELLS & WHISTLES

"*T*revionnn!"

Royelle jumped up, screaming out his name in hysterics sweating from head to toe. The beautiful dream turned nightmare caused her to fight in her sleep while trying to catch her breath. She felt like demons were riding her chest, trying to suck the air out of her. She frantically looked around the room to see if he was around, but the room was still quiet and bland as hell. It had a strange eerie feel to it and emptied of all things Trevion related, including his permanent scent, which had faded away.

While she was no expert in the field of dreams, she knew there was a significant meaning behind hers. She quickly grabbed her phone, checking to see if he had tried to reach out; there was nothing. Yet, even with the melancholy dream leaving her with an uneasy spirit, she was more than willing to let this cut burn.

After all that she had learned about him, she couldn't even fathom the idea of calling him. She was so disgusted by him that the mere thought of reaching out first, as she had always done in the past, completely nauseated her. He did the damage; therefore, she felt it was his responsibility to extend himself to her and do the mending first for a change.

Once she regulated her breathing and heart rate, she blankly stared up at the ceiling, trying to determine what she would deal with first when she got to work. Monday's were the fucking pits at the office. It was back to the basics of dealing with funky-ass McKenzie and clients who somehow always found themselves on the opposite side of the law. Allowing the contamination of Trevion's fraudulence interfere with her routine was not an option.

"Urgh. This quietness is depressing. But you got what you wanted, didn't you?" She asked herself, looking around the lifeless room.

She pulled the sheets from around her body and swung her feet over to the side of the bed. She took a good hard look at the 8x11 wedding photo of her and Trevion that sat on the nightstand and didn't know whether to cry or smile. There were happier moments depicted in the photo, but the void in the house served as a dig in the ribs, that the picture was a façade and a thing of the past.

"Wowww!" She shook her head.

She was in disbelief that the man she was so deeply in love with was the same man that she kicked out, had to question everything about, and it scorched her soul something awful. When she stood up to go into her master bathroom, her ceiling to floor corner mirror stopped her naked reflection dead in her tracks. She stood still, looking at her likeness, never realizing that all the stress from everything she was going through was starting to take an unpleasant toll on her. She was sure that her mother slowly dying had a lot to do with it but attributed the remaining of her weight loss and sunken eyes to everything she was going through with Trevion.

"Come on, Royelle Amoire. Get yourself together, girl. You are better than this."

Realizing that she was letting herself go behind, all the bullshit between her and Trevion got to her mentally. It was the first time that she realized he had truly broken her. Everything good in her, he had taken from her. And while she enjoyed being with AJ, looking back at herself in the mirror made her feel like shit. Despite all of Trevion's lies and deception, she knew two wrongs didn't make a right.

The fact remained, she still wasn't 100% sure of all of Trevion's wrongs. All she had was the sticky note she found near her bathroom floor and the ones inside the book that she was trying to compare to an Excel spreadsheet. As far as she was concerned, that wasn't enough to say that Trevion was doing anything other than having a few side hustles of sorts.

She had a tough time believing that Trevion could ever do what she and Xandra suspected him of doing. Selling her for sex right under her nose didn't seem plausible. And while it was hard for her to accept the truth of it all, she still wasn't willing to budge for him. She swore that she wouldn't accept his calls, see him, or welcome him back to the house until he came clean about everything. It was a tough decision for her to make, but it was necessary.

As she began walking toward the bathroom, she heard loud bangs coming from the downstairs area. She paused for a moment to make sure she wasn't tripping, and a few seconds later, she heard the loud knocks again. She quickly grabbed her mini robe and hurried down the stairs when she heard the loud knocking again for the third time.

"Dag nab it! I'm coming!" She yelled.

She couldn't wait to see who it was at her door being disruptive at seven in the morning. And when she looked out the peephole, she was surprised to see a Caucasian and African American man in their nicely pressed suits with shiny gold badges dangling over their lapels standing outside her door. When she opened it, they could tell that she was irritated and disgusted with their early morning unsolicited wake-up call.

"Yes! Can I help you gentleman with something?" She sassed, with a croaky voice wiping the sleep out of her eyes.

"Royelle Blevins?"

"Kingsley." She corrected. "What can I help you gentleman with?"

"My name is Detective Presley, and this is my partner Detective Aveen. May we come in for a moment, please?"

Royelle frowned. "May I ask what this is about? I've already answered all the questions I could with the other two detectives."

"Ma'am?" Detective Aveen was confused.

"Detective Blackthorn and Rowley. I've already answered all their

6

questions down at the station and provided them with whatever information I could."

"Ma'am, please. May we?" Detective Presley urged.

Royelle sucked her teeth, "Sure." She hesitantly responded.

She unlocked the screen door in an ill-natured manner, let the detectives into her home, and guided them to the family room to have a seat.

"Please give me a moment to put on some decent clothes and wash my face."

"By all means, ma'am. Take your time." Detective Aveen responded.

Royelle went into her room huffing and puffing, grabbed whatever bra, T-shirt, and pajama pants she could find, and quickly got dressed. She went into the bathroom, brushed her teeth, washed her face, and pulled her back into a ponytail.

As the detectives waited, they took note of how clean the house was and smelled. Their job was to inspect everything within eyeshot and make sure that nothing appeared to be amiss. They looked at all the pictures of her and Trevion on their wedding day and from their vacations. They also noted her pictures with Xandra, her brother, sister, and mother; there were none of Rayford.

"Thank you for waiting. What can I help you with?" Royelle asked upon returning.

"Thank you, ma'am." Both detectives responded in one pitch.

"No problem. I mean, I already told the other two that I wasn't here the day Mrs. Benton— Well, you know."

The detectives both gave a slight nod.

"We understand." Detective Presley responded.

"As I explained to the other detectives, my job can account for my whereabouts on that day. I voluntarily went down to the station and gave my statement to be helpful, not so that it would make me a suspect. Surely you can understand why I am a little frustrated by your presence here today about this, at seven in the morning, no less."

The detectives looked at each other with a slack expression as Royelle continued to speak, not allowing them a minute to interrupt.

"And ma'am, we appreciate you doing that. However, we are here on a separate matter altogether." Detective Aveen said.

"Oh? About what?" She asked, surprised.

They had finally gotten her attention.

"We'd like to ask you a few questions about Trevion Kingsley."

"Trevion? You all are not here on the matter surrounding Mrs. Benton?" She asked confusingly.

"No, ma'am." Detective Aveen responded.

"Okkk…Well, what about him? Is he ok? Is he in jail?" Royelle anxiously asked.

"Can you tell us what your relationship is to him and how long you all have known each other?" Detective Presley asked.

Royelle paused for a moment and swallowed the knot that expeditiously developed in her throat. Being an employee at the law firm, she was familiar with specific lines of questioning, and these questions made her stomach churn, causing her to get nauseous and making her heart beat a little faster.

"Officers, please! Tell me what this is about. Please do not undermine my ability to understand where this is going. I am a Paralegal. I work for the Premiere Law Offices, and I know an interrogation when I feel and smell one coming on, not to mention when I'm in the middle of one."

"Ma'am. This is not an interrogation. We are just asking basic questions at the moment." Detective Aveen affirmed.

"I understand that. But why?" She quickly snapped back.

"The moment you answer our questions, we will be more than happy to answer yours." Detective Presley replied, now playing hardball.

"Ok. Fine! I've been with Trevion for five years, and we've been married for one."

"Where were you on the night of August 24th?" Detective Presley continued.

"What? Why?"

Royelle grew hot and was getting angrier and angrier by the second. She couldn't believe that she was being interrogated about Trevion and not Mrs. Benton. It didn't make sense why they were asking her those kinds of questions about him. And detective Presley being a complete dick towards her wasn't helping.

"Ma'am. Please just answer the question." Detective Presley said.

Royelle rolled her neck and looked directly at Detective Presley with stark eyes. "That was two nights ago. I was at my sister Xandra's house with my friend Ajah. They can both confirm it."

"And what time would you say you left from there?"

"I had fallen asleep on Xandra's couch and got home around seven something the following morning. But, again, both she and Ajah can account for that."

"This relationship with Trevion, would you say it's authentic?" Detective Presley hounded.

"Authentic?! What kind of question is that?! Of course, it is! Listen!" Royelle stood up in a rage, wiping her tears. "I am not sure what you all are eluding to, but I am not answering any more questions until you tell me why you are here."

"Ma'am, this would be more fitting down at the station so that we can get your full statement recorded." Detective Aveen remarked.

"Really?! Full statement?! You all come here at seven in the morning, with all your bells and whistles type of questions lined up, wake me out of my sleep, rudely, might I add, question me in my house about my husband, and still refuse to tell me why or if he's even ok! Some nerve you all have! Gentlemen, it's time for you all to leave, and I am not asking!"

Royelle walked to the front door, opened it, and waited for them to march out of her house.

"Ma'am, it's important for you to come to the police station. If you don't, you'll be forcing us to come back." Detective Presley informed.

"Oh! Don't worry! I'll be there!"

"With an attorney too." Detective Presely snickered while passing her his business card.

"Oh! You bet your ass!" She snapped back, snatching the card out of his hand.

She slammed the door and quickly ran upstairs to get her cell phone. She didn't know whether to be mad or continue to cry. She hadn't spoken to Trevion since she kicked him out, so she had no idea what he had been doing or where he was staying. But after what had just transpired, the being mad act was out the window; she needed to be sure he was ok. So she called his phone, and it went straight to voicemail. She tried a few more times and got the same result. She was peeved! He wasn't answering, and she was clueless about what was happening.

The tiny bit of family she knew he had, lived out of state, so she didn't bother calling them. She was confident they wouldn't know what had happened or what was happening anyway. She tried calling Xandra, and her phone went straight to voicemail as well. She didn't know what to do. Putting Raymelle or Raylina in her business was a no-go. Therefore, she called the last person she knew she could trust.

"Good Morning, Royelle."

"Good Morning. I need your help!" She said ecstatically.

"Calm down. What's wrong?"

"Charlyn, I need an attorney."

"For what?! What happened, Royelle?" Charlyn frantically asked.

"I don't know. Detectives came to my house asking me questions about Trevion, wouldn't tell me why, and told me to come down to the station."

"Ok. Take a deep breath. It's probably nothing to be concerned with. What station do we need to go to?" Charlyn asked.

"I believe Stoughton, but just be sure...." Royelle grabbed Detective Presley's card off the bed.

"Milton?! She yelled. "Why in the hell would I have to go to Milton?!" She continued.

"Royelleee... Calm down. It could have been a basic traffic stop; who knows. You know we've fought many cases for people of color in Milton. DWB. But I don't have to tell or explain that to you because you already know."

Charlyn was trying to stay as optimistic as she could be for the sake of Royelle. But, knowing the law as well as she did, she knew the reasoning behind two detectives going to Royelle's home to question her about anything was far more profound than a routine traffic stop.

"I know this is asking a lot of you, Charlyn."

"Nonsense!" She interrupted. "I told you before, I'm not your mother but can advise and guide you like one. Let me call the office and arrange for McKenzie to cancel my morning."

"I'm so sorry, Charlyn, but I had no one else to turn to."

"You did the right thing, Royelle. It's all right."

"What time should I meet you at the station?" Royelle asked.

"I can be there by Nine. And Royelle..." Charlyn paused.

"Yes, ma'am."

"Take it easy. We will get to the bottom of all of this. I promise you."

"Yes, ma'am. Thank you."

Royelle disconnected the call and attempted Xandra's phone again with the same voicemail result. She sucked her teeth, threw her phone on the bed, and jumped in the shower. She was perplexed. The visit was so rude and abrupt, and the information they refused to give her left her trying to decide whether she was coming or going. It was hard for her to make heads or tails of what might have happened to him or what kind of trouble he was mixed up in. Despite this, she was determined to get down to the station, clear things up, and get her husband out of the forbidden hands of the Milton police department.

Soon as she was done showering, she checked her phone to see if anyone had returned her calls, but there was nothing. Finally, with less than an hour to burn, she decided to pray. The presence of God was the only thing that could calm her worried, troubled, and disquieted spirit. As she got into a kneeling position, she remembered the words of her mother's nurse, Suzanne, from a while back...

"God is a God of restoration, conviction, love, and truth, and will always be available to you. If there is a truth you are seeking, he will reveal it. If it's deliverance from something, he will make it happen. If you're missing love, he will provide it. If you're feeling lonely, he will hold you. Just hold onto him. He has you right in the palm of his hands. Seek God in all things."

As soon as she was done remembering those words and praying, she stood to her feet, put on her armor of strength, gathered her things, and walked out the door.

11

CHAPTER 2:
REALITY SWITCH

As she began her drive down to Milton, everything was fuzzy to her. It was hard for her to wrap her mind around the idea that Trevion could have done anything besides speeding while driving through Milton. It frustrated her that the detectives weren't forthcoming. But she knew that whatever it was, Charlyn would handle them one way or another. She didn't play about her reputation as an attorney, and she damn sure didn't play about her staff, particularly Royelle.

Royelle had the right mind to call Xandra again, but Xandra's derision about the police, her reluctance to go with her when she had to give a recorded statement on Mrs. Benton, her always ghetto, and always on the defense attitude deterred Royelle from making the call. She needed to stay calm, and Xandra was the complete opposite of that whenever it involved the police.

As Royelle approached the station, she started to get bubble guts. Her hands were trembling, her heart was racing, and her mouth was watering from the nauseous and anxious feeling she was experiencing. It was such an uneasy energy. It reminded her of the time the doctor's called in a family meeting to discuss and confirm Adala's official diagnosis. She wanted to never experience that feeling ever again in life, but so it was. The feeling had resurfaced, and it was just as disturbing at this moment as it was back then.

Royelle made it to the station five minutes before the scheduled meet time, and Charlyn was already sitting in the front lobby. Judging from Royelle's somber and drab-looking face, Charlyn could tell that Royelle had a rough morning, and she secretly prayed that the mishap with Trevion was just that; a minor mishap.

With Royelle's mother at Angel Zone facing death any day, her father being the dick he was, the unsolved murder of Mrs. Benton, and Trevion's treacherous ways, there was no telling how much more Royelle could take. Charlyn was sure that if the detectives had anything to discuss more significant than a misdemeanor, it would throw Royelle into a suicidal cyclone.

"Good Morning, Charlyn." Royelle greeted.

"Good Morning, sweetie." Charlyn stood up and hugged her. "Are you ok? You don't look so good."

"I'm ok. Just tired and ready to get to the bottom of whatever this is."

"Of course. Well, they already know that I am here on your behalf. We were just waiting for you. Are you ready?"

"I am, but I can't lie. This makes me nervous."

"I understand. But let's not assume anything. Let's just get in there and hear what they have to say."

Charlyn walked over to the desk and informed the female uniformed officer that they were ready to meet with Detective Presley and Aveen. Quickly after she made the call, Detective Aveen came out and escorted the women to the back.

"Good morning, ladies." He greeted softly.

"Good morning," Charlyn replied. Royelle didn't say a word.

"Follow me this way." Detective Aveen said.

As they walked through the halls to the back, where the interrogation rooms were located, Royelle looked around with a flat look on her face. The building wasn't anything like the one she had been to when giving her statement for Mrs. Benton's murder. Instead, this building was monotonous and depressing. She could only imagine how the inmates felt while they were in their cells, particularly the inmates of color.

13

When they made it to the small square room, her eyes opened wide. She couldn't believe that she was walking into a room that looked like something out of the sixties; the only exception, the chairs weren't bolted to the floor. There were no windows, no sunlight, and the 4x6 table that sat in the middle of the room, accompanied by four chairs, was big enough to fit four people, maybe five if they stayed standing. The cameras in the upper right and left-hand corners that she knew were recording their every move made her feel like a suspect instead of a concerned wife.

"Good Morning all." Detective Presley greeted.

Again, Royelle said nothing. She didn't care for him at all. His disposition towards her earlier put a bad taste in her mouth. At this point, she had no energy left to give him. She took more to Detective Aveen, who seemed to have a more compassionate temperament. She couldn't tell if it was the good cop, bad cop routine, but if it was, it wasn't hard to figure out who was who.

"Gentlemen, my name is Charlyn Richardson, Senior Attorney at the Premiere Law Offices, representing Royelle Kingsley." She handed each of them her business card.

"Nice to meet you, counselor. The reason we asked Mrs. Blevins down here—" Detective Presley started.

"Kingsley." Royelle corrected.

"Ma'am?" Detective Presley asked.

"Kingsley. My last name is Kingsley. Why do you insist on addressing me incorrectly?" She peevishly asked.

"My apologies." He shrewdly responded. "Mrs. Kingsley, we asked you down here to get a formal statement.

"A formal statement about what?" Royelle spat.

When Charlyn felt the heat spewing from Royelle, she quickly grabbed her left hand and gently squeezed it. It was Charlyn's way of trying to keep Royelle calm and avoiding the interview from ending before it even started.

"Detectives. Please. Let's get on with it. Just ask what you need to ask." Charlyn stiffly redirected.

Detective Presley cut his eyes at Charlyn and turned his attention back towards Royelle.

14

"Mrs. Kingsley, some of these questions you have already answered at your home. But for the record, we need to ask them again."

"Fine." She rolled her eyes.

The detectives began with the same fundamental questions they had previously asked, and she answered each one no different than she did the first time.

"You told us earlier how long you and Trevion have been together, but can you tell us how the two of you met?"

"What does that question have to do with why he's here?" Royelle asked in an affronted tone.

"I understand it may sound like a silly question, but it's necessary." Detective Presley said.

Royelle looked over at Charlyn for guidance, and she gave Royelle a head nod signifying it was ok for her to answer the question. Royelle rolled her eyes again and turned back toward the detectives.

"We met five years ago when I was on my way home from a class.

"Would you say that your relationship is healthy?

"What?!" Royelle chuckled. "What does it matter? This is ridiculous! Charlyn?"

Royelle looked back over at Charlyn, and again, she approved by giving the same head nod she did moments before.

"Our marriage is fine." Royelle snapped.

"What about money issues?" Detective Presley asked.

"What about them? We have none. He owns his business, and I work hard. All of our bills are paid, and we are not in any debt. Our marriage is fine. We are fine."

Royelle paused for a second, death-starred the detectives down, then looked over at Charlyn as an alarming sensation came over her.

"Where is Trevion?! I'm not answering any more questions about myself, Trevion, or our lives until I know what's going on with him!" She yelled.

"Detectives, my client is within her rights. So what's the purpose of the visit?" Charlyn demanded answers.

"Royelle." Detective Aveen spoke softly.

15

"Sir. Do not Royelle me unless the next thing coming out of your mouth is attached to an explanation."

Royelle was trying to remain in control and keep calm, but she was at her wit's end, and her attitude had reached a peak that surpassed the way she generally carried herself.

"Mrs. Kingsley, please," Detective Aveen calmly spoke again.

"I'm listening." She snapped.

He was trying to keep her calm, but she was done playing nice by this time, so he had no other choice than to just say what needed to be said.

"The reason we called you here was not only to get more information on Trevion but also to inform you that he was shot and pronounced dea—"

Instantly everything around Royelle went blank. She could feel the ashy blue walls turn dark and cave in around her while the dirty ceramic floor collapsed from under her feet. She heard nothing but a hollow ringing pitch in the center of her ears. Royelle was frozen, rooted in place. Her heart was rapidly skipping beats resembling that of a murmur, and her stomach twisted in painful knots as if she had eaten a poisonous forbidden fruit. Her folded hands were clenched together so tight that her fingernail plates turned White, losing their natural Pink color. Remembering how to breathe passed her by as she heaved heavily in and out, trying to catch her breath and cope with the news that she didn't let Detective Aveen finish giving her.

"Royelle!" Charlyn snapped her fingers.

With an anguished look, Royelle slowly looked over at Charlyn.

"Royelle. Look at me." Charlyn said in a soft tone.

Charlyn had never seen Royelle in such a state of mind. It was frightening to witness how empty she had quickly become. The detectives, however, sat, watched, and took mental notes of every reaction she displayed. It took a few minutes for everything to register, but as soon as Royelle let Detective Aveen's words pierce through her soul, she let out a howling cry that could be heard throughout the entire station.

"This can't be! This can't be!" She yelled.

"Royelle." Charlyn softly spoke again, trying not to agitate her any further.

"No, Charlyn!" Royelle jumped up out of her seat. "I demand to see my husband right now!" She screamed.

The detectives stayed seated and patiently waited for her to realize they weren't playing.

"Royelle, please."

Charlyn stood up, grabbed Royelle's hands, pulled her in closer, and hugged her tightly while her tears soaked through Charlyn's White button-down blouse. Royelle's cries were heart-wrenching. The affliction she was experiencing, everyone in the room felt. Even the seasoned detectives who were conditioned to have no sympathy for potential murder suspects could tell that she was in a state of shock and defiled agony. That was just the first blow. They hated to see how she was going to react to the next.

"Detectives, I think that's enough for now. I need to get Mrs. Kingsley home."

"No!" Royelle raised up from Charlyn's shoulder. "I'm not leaving until they tell me where my husband is!" She looked at both detectives with piercing fiery eyes.

"Royelle, please be seated." Detective Aveen said.

"No! I want to see my husband! Where is he?!" She continued to yell.

"Royelle, please be seated." He pleaded again.

She backed up against the wall and crossed her arms. "I'm not sitting! I'm ready to leave, and you need to tell me where he is now!" Royelle aggressively demanded.

"Mrs. Kingsley, we can't do that." Detective Aveen responded.

"What?!" Royelle yelled.

"And why not, detective?" Charlyn questioned.

"Unfortunately, Mrs. Kingsley was not listed as his next of kin."

"What the hell are you talking about?! I'm his wife and the only one that would be listed as his next of kin!"

"I'm sorry, detectives. I don't understand." Charlyn said.

"Mrs. Kingsley is not listed—"

"Detective Aveen!" Charlyn spoke harshly. "I heard you the first time. So, who ID'ed him." She grilled.

"Hospital records had someone else listed as his next of kin; that's all I can tell you."

17

"So, who was it?!" Royelle yelled.

"Ma'am, please have a seat."

"Gawt damn it! Who was it?!" Royelle hollered.

"I'm not at liberty to say." Detective Aveen said calmly.

"That's bullshit, and you know it!" Charlyn spoke out. "This is his wife, and she's entitled to all the information you have on him, including the person listed as his next of kin. And if you don't, I will report you to—"

"Counselor!" Detective Presley cut her off. "I see that the reality switch is officially on here. And what we're trying to explain is that Trevion had someone else listed as his wife and next of kin at the hospital. Royelle was not that person, nor was she listed anywhere on the hospital documents."

"What?! That's bullshit!" Royelle screamed with her eyes bulging.

"I'm afraid not, ma'am. We investigated and confirmed it before we contacted you. Now we understand this is a lot to take in, but this is the reason we had you come down here." Detective Presley continued.

"This is a fucking joke!" Royelle blurted out. "This has to be a fucking joke! Charlyn, let's go!"

Royelle opened the door and tried to find her way to the exit, but her clouded mind couldn't remember the direction.

"Royelle, wait!" Charlyn yelled, running up to her. "It's this way." She grabbed Royelle's right hand, redirected her, and walked with her out the front door.

Charlyn released her grip, and Royelle began walking about in a haze. She couldn't decipher if what was happening was real or if she was in the same dream that had turned dark hours earlier. Whatever it was, it was eating her alive inside out.

Charlyn tried to talk some sense into her as they stood outside the station, but none of it was registering. Royelle looked right through her. It was as if she was peering through a two-way mirror. She could hear and see Charlyn but wasn't sure if Charlyn could *really* see her— the shock, the confusion, the hurt, the pain, and the rage that she was in. She didn't know whether to hate Trevion more for the fraudulent marriage or love him harder because he was dead. Both carried the exact same burden. After a few minutes of listening to and staring at Charlyn, Royelle took off running towards her car, trying as fast as she could to get away from the station.

"Royelle! Stop!" Charlyn yelled.

Charlyn wouldn't dare run after her in her six-inch Bergdorf Goodman heels, and Royelle could care less if she did. All she saw was Red. Nothing mattered; no one mattered. Royelle was on a mission. Charlyn was still a reasonable distance away from Royelle but could see her head jolting up and down. She couldn't tell what was happening but knew it couldn't be anything good.

"Royelleee! Stoppp! What are you doing?!" She yelled as she got visibly closer.

She ran towards her, baffled to see Royelle banging her forehead on the driver's side door. When she grabbed Royelle's arm, forcing her to turn around, her heavy breathing, the way her chest was falling and rising, the hollow look in her eyes, and the wildness of her hair sent a chill through Charlyn. It put her in the mind of Drew Barrymore from the movie Firestarter. She couldn't believe what she was seeing. But one thing was certain—Royelle had checked out.

"Royelle!"

Royelle blankly stared at her.

"Royelle, listen to me!" Charlyn shook her hard.

"Charlyn." Royelle heaved. "Get. Out. Of. My. Way!"

Royelle's stern, deep, and unrecognizable voice sent a frightening chill through Charlyn.

"Royelle, please." Charlyn pleaded.

Royelle turned around, unlocked her door, and jumped in her car. The sounds of Charlyn begging her not to leave were all but clear. The only thing replaying in Royelle's ear waves at this point were the words, *Trevion's dead* and *married to someone else.*

CHAPTER 3:
SNAPPED

*I*t surprised and angered Charlyn to see that none of the police officers in the parking lot, including the two who interrogated Royelle, tried to render aid. None of them tried to stop her, or follow behind them, even when they saw Royelle exhibiting erratic behavior before she sped out of the lot. It was a recipe for disaster waiting to happen.

Milton's narrow residential streets were not made for the 70 to 80 miles an hour Royelle was pushing. And the fact that she had no destination in mind and showed no signs of slowing down made Charlyn very nervous. She continuously tried to call Royelle on her cell phone, and since she wouldn't answer, Charlyn had no other choice but to call for help.

"911. What is your emergency?" The dispatcher answered.

"Yes. I am on Canton Ave, near the Milton Police Department on Highland Ave. I am following one of my employees, who is driving negligently and at high speed. She needs help before she hurts herself or someone else." Charlyn spoke as calmly and professionally as she could.

"Ma'am, what is your precise location?"

"I-I-I don't know." She stuttered. "I just know we are on Canton Ave right now." She continued as her eyes began to water.

"What is your employee's name?"

"Royelle Kingsley."

"Can you tell me the make and model of the car?"

"It's a Candy Red Genesis. License Plate TKJK 1113."

"We have patrols on the way. I'm going to stay on the line with you so that I can update them as you update me."

"Yes, ma'am. Thank you.

"Where are you currently?"

"We are on…"

Before Charlyn could say anything else, the dispatcher could vaguely hear the screeching of tires followed by Charlyn's screams.

"Ma'am, what's going on?" She concernedly asked.

"Get help here quick! Charlyn yelled.

"Ma'am! What's happening!"

"She just crashed into a tree! Get an ambulance here now!" Charlyn threw her phone down, put her car in park, and ran to Royelle's car.

"Ma'am, are you there?! Can you hear me?" The dispatcher asked.

As soon as she realized that Charlyn was no longer responding, she alerted the police that it was no longer just a speeding vehicle call, but an accident and quickly dispatched the EMTs. And when Charlyn got to Royelle's car, her mouth dropped. She didn't even recognize it. Except for the rear, everything in the front was mangled. There was no way she could get to Royelle.

"Royelle! Can you hear me?! She yelled.

Royelle was knocked out. It was clear to everyone standing by that she was unconscious. The impact was so disastrous that everyone looking on, including Charlyn, suspected Royelle might be dead.

"Ma'am, are you ok? We're getting you all some help." One of the bystanders said.

Charlyn was such a mess, she couldn't even respond. She stood in shock trying to process what had just happened. Things had gone from sugar to shit real quick. As if things couldn't get any worse for the Blevins family, now Charlyn had the task of adding more bad news.

"Clear the area, everybody! Please, everybody, step back!" One of the

Troopers hollered, running towards the car to assess the damage.

Charlyn was so zoned out she never heard the sirens or realized that she was standing as close to the passenger side as she was just sobbing. And while she knew better than to blame herself for what was happening, she somehow felt slightly responsible as she looked on in stupefaction at what she saw as Royelle's motionless body. She couldn't tell if Royelle was breathing, alive, or what. There was blood everywhere, and she couldn't see past that.

"Ma'am, I'm gonna need you to come with me." The female state trooper placed her arm around Charlyn's shoulders and guided her away from the crash site.

As the other officers and state police secured the accident scene with yellow tape pushing the bystanders back, the female statey placed Charlyn in her cruiser giving her some time to calm down and collect her thoughts. She needed Charlyn focused so she could gather as much information as she could.

"My name is State Trooper Wright. Do you want a bottle of water?" She kindly asked.

"No." Charlyn cried.

"Can you tell me what happened here today?"

"Is she ok?" Charlyn asked, ignoring the trooper's question.

"I don't know yet. But I need to ask you some questions while everything is still fresh in your mind."

"I understand." Charlyn sadly responded.

She did understand, but she didn't give a shit about what Trooper Wright was talking about. She needed to know that Royelle was ok. But she also knew that the longer it took her to answer the questions, the longer it was going to take for her to get to Royelle. Charlyn took a deep breath and gave a detailed account from the beginning of the day up until the very moment they left the police station.

Being an attorney, she knew the importance of glorifying stories. And although she was unsure of Royelle's status, she still wanted to paint a picture for the trooper in a way that would make them feel some sympathy towards Royelle's irrepressible behavior in case they felt the need to charge her with something later on.

"Can you tell me what you saw right before the accident?"

"As I told the dispatcher, I was concerned because her driving was nomadic, directionless, and I couldn't stop her. What's more alarming is that the Milton police saw her drive out of their parking lot in a volatile way and did nothing. That says a lot about their level of concern, and I will be filing a complaint against them." She added as if the statey cared.

"Do you know how fast she was going?"

"I would say probably 65 miles per hour. I honestly don't know. I'm just guessing."

Charlyn knew it was much faster than that, but she didn't want to incriminate herself or Royelle, for that matter.

"Do you know if something crossed in front of her, or maybe she was distracted by something else that would've caused her to crash?"

"I honestly do not know. All I remember was driving down Canton Ave and going up Centre street. When she made the left, she lost control of the car, hit that small stone wall back there, and then the tree that the car is resting at now.".

"Is there anything else you can remember or tell me that might be helpful?"

"No. That's everything."

Charlyn turned around just in time to see the EMTs closing the doors to the ambulance.

"Wait! Where are they taking her?" She anxiously asked, getting out of the cruiser trying to catch the ambulance before it pulled off.

"Ma'am!" Trooper Wright hollered.

Charlyn absently starred at the ambulance as it drove away. And as professional as she was most days, this situation left her completely debilitated.

"Ma'am!" Trooper Wright yelled again, signaling for Charlyn to walk towards her.

"Please tell me she's ok," Charlyn said as she got closer.

"I don't have that information, but she's going to BMC. You can meet her there."

"Thank you! Thank you!"

"Here's my card in case you need anything."

Charlyn snatched the card out of her hand, ran to her car as fast as she could, and grabbed her phone.

"Trooper Wright!" She yelled out.

Trooper Wright turned around, and the two began walking towards each other.

"If it's not too much to ask. I need to get pictures of the car. Can I take pictures? Or could you, since I can't go past the yellow tape?"

"I'm not supposed to, but given the circumstances..."

She took Charlyn's phone, got as close as she could to the car, and took several pictures.

"I hope this helps your purpose."

"It will."

Charlyn grabbed her phone, ran back to the car, and peeled off, heading for Boston Medical Center.

CHAPTER 4:

UNCONSCIOUS

"Registration, you have an ambulance!" The woman loudly said on the overhead speaker.

When Royelle arrived, a whole team of nurses and doctors who were already briefed on her condition were waiting on her arrival with the anticipation that they'd have their work cut out for them.

"This is Royelle Kingsley." The female EMT spoke.

"She's going into room three!" One of the nurses yelled out.

The nurse led the way, and everyone followed. With Royelle being unconscious and given the information about her accident, head trauma and internal bleeding were their primary concern. They had to act fast. As the nurses were working double time hooking Royelle to IVs, intubating her, and drawing a full panel of blood, Dr. Pisces opened Royelle's eyes one by one, checking to see if her pupils would constrict; and they did. She raised Royelle's arms and legs, and they each fell without restraint and hesitation. She called out to Royelle and didn't get any verbal or visual response.

"We need to get her down for a head and brain MRI STAT!" Dr. Pisces hollered. "I also want a CT of her AB & Pelvis with and without! Does anyone know if she's here with somebody?!"

"No, ma'am. There was a woman at the scene with her, but she was being questioned by Troopers when we left. The male EMT responded.

"Somebody let the front know I want to see that person when and if she arrives!"

"Yes, Doctor." The triage registration nurse replied.

There was never a dull moment to be had at BMC, and one would be a fool to look for one. While all the commotion was going on in the back surrounding Royelle, the front of the ER had its own set of madness to conquer. Several meth mile patients were coming in and out, looking for relief. Other patients were checking in for different emergency reasons, while others were stopping by patient relations looking for the room numbers of their family and friends. It was a damn zoo in the front lobby.

"Hello, sir. How can I help you?" The woman at the patient information desk asked.

"My name is Detective Aveen." He brandished his badge. "Is Royelle Kingsley here?"

"Just a moment." The patient representative said.

She quickly looked for her name in the EPIC database, and it didn't show that she was a current patient. The registration nurses in the back had yet to update all of Royelle's information; therefore, nothing was showing up on the registration log for the front desk.

"I'm sorry, sir. No one by that name has checked in."

"Are you sure? Could you double-check? She would've come by ambulance."

"Sure." She replied.

Rather than recheck the computer, she got up and went to the back where the E.R. rooms were.

As Detective Aveen stood there waiting, Charlyn came rushing through the doors like a bat out of hell, looking like complete shit. She brushed past Detective Aveen, never noticing that he was standing right next to her.

"Ma'am! I need to know if Royelle Kingsley has arrived yet?!" She said out of breath as the woman walked back towards her desk.

"Counselor?" The Detective had a puzzled look on his face.

He looked her up and down, shocked to see her looking the way she was. Just an hour before, she was well put together, looking like an attorney no one wanted to fuck with. Now she looked like someone who had just escaped her captor.

"My apologies, Detective. She is here. You can both follow me."

She walked them to the back and left them in the quiet room that would soon be Royelle's. Charlyn sat down and let out a huge sigh. She wasn't only worried about Royelle's medical condition, but she was hurting for her emotional and mental state too.

"I'm sorry about all of this." Detective Aveen said, breaking the silence.

"You should be. You all saw Royelle's condition and did nothing to help. This is all on you. What did you think was going to happen with that kind of news detective? For a guilty person, it may have gone over differently. But for someone like Royelle, we'll be lucky if she makes it out of this alive or if she will ever be the same again. Even for me, that was a hard blow, and I'm not in her shoes. But, enough of that. Off the record, do you really think she had anything to do with his murder?"

"Off the record. No. I don't. But we can't rule it out either."

Charlyn rolled her eyes.

"Detective. Royelle is incapable of murder. She has worked for me for nearly six years, and up until today, I've never seen her get a wrinkle on her forehead from being angry or upset. She couldn't harm a fly, let alone someone she is completely in love with."

"That may be true. But understand, like you, we have a job to do too."

"Do your due diligence. But, just know, I can more than guarantee you won't find anything on her, not so much as a damn traffic ticket."

As Charlyn looked away from Detective Aveen, Dr. Pisces walked in, blocking him from seeing Charlyn's tears. She was strong and dangerous in and out of court but letting anyone see her weakness was out of the question.

"Hello, I'm Dr. Pisces, head E.R. doctor." She kindly said, sticking her right hand out to shake theirs. "It's my understanding that Mrs. Kingsley may have suffered a psychotic break after learning some devasting news of her husband? Is that right?" Dr. Pisces asked.

"I guess you can call it that. It all happened so fast. Once she got the news from this detective and his partner, she left the police station driving extremely fast and crashed into a tree moments later. By the time I reached the car, she appeared to be unconscious." Charlyn answered with contempt towards the detective.

"I understand. Well, based on the preliminary assessments I did of Royelle when she arrived, it looks like she may have suffered some head trauma. It's still hard to tell how much or how serious without running the necessary tests. I sent her down for a head and brain MRI and a CT Scan of her Abdomen and Pelvis. This is all to rule out any internal injury or bleeding. And also to see what her brain activity is or isn't showing."

"Is she responsive at all?" Charlyn asked.

"No. Not at this tiome. Her vitals are ok, but I will know more once we see all the results. At which point, the Neurology team will be down to meet with you all to discuss all the facts."

Charlyn had no words. She silently cried on the inside.

"Are you family?" Dr. Pisces asked.

"Not technically. I'm her boss."

"Ok. That's not a problem. However, the Neuro team is going to need to speak with her next of kin once everything comes back. Will you be able to get in contact with them?"

"That won't be a problem," Charlyn responded.

In the meantime, just press the red buzzer on the remote if either of you needs anything."

The doctor walked out of the room, and Charlyn directed her attention back towards Detective Aveen.

"Well, Detective. You heard it here first. We're going to be here awhile. Therefore, anything you need from Royelle regarding your case will have to take a backseat."

"Seems so…for now. I just wanted to be sure that she'd be ok."

"She's a fighter. She'll get through this. In the meantime, when she is fully awake, able, and willing to talk to you all again, I'll be sure to contact you." Charlyn snarled.

"Here's my card just in case you lost the other one in the shuffle."

He placed the card on the food tray table and walked out of the room.

Charlyn quickly jumped up and went after him.

"Detective." She called out.

"Counselor?" He turned around.

"Are you sure about the wife thing?"

"As sure as I am that this suit is a Black Ralph Lauren."

"Thank you," Charlyn said.

She turned around and walked back into the room. She sat down, took a deep breath, called her office, and had her assistant Jacob pull Royelle's emergency contacts from her file.

CHAPTER 5:
SISTER

*W*ith all nine hoops in the gym at the YMCA being occupied by different people screeching the floors with their sneakers, and yelling about who to throw the ball to, who to cover, or who to play defense against, Raymelle couldn't hear the back to back calls that Charlyn was placing trying to get a hold of him. After so many failed attempts, she finally left him a voicemail leaving little details, hoping not to alarm him too much.

She tried reaching Raylina, but the number Royelle had listed for her was disconnected. Given that she knew Xandra wasn't her biological sister and her knowledge of the hostility between Royelle and her father, she felt it best to let Raymelle or Raylina contact them instead. While she waited for Raymelle to call back, she sat quietly, replaying all the times she and Royelle talked about her and Trevion from the beginning of their marriage up until the very moment at the police station.

Relating to some of Royelle's pain was easy. She knew about the heartbreak that came from a cheating spouse, but a cheating dead spouse, now that was different. She couldn't even begin to understand what those two combinations of torment felt like. To help pass the time, she started scrolling through some of the online news channels and different social media feeds to see if anything had been reported about Trevion or the accident, but there was nothing. The last thing she wanted was for Royelle's family to hear about it from the news, social media, or strangers rather than hearing it from someone they knew. And when Raymelle finally called, she was happier than a pig in shit.

"Hello?" Charlyn whispered into the phone.

"Charlyn, it's Raymelle. I just got your message. Now, what's going on with my sister?" He worriedly asked, disregarding her greeting.

"I'm not sure what's going on with her yet. The doctors are running some tests on her."

"Ok. But why is she even there in the first place?"

Charlyn took a deep breath before answering.

"She was in a car accident. You should get down to the hospital as soon as you can, honey."

"Accident?! Man! What hospital y'all at?!"

"We're at BMC."

"I'm on my way!

Raymelle disconnected the call and quickly started stuffing all his belongings into his gym bag. Without explanation to his boys, Raymelle chucked them the deuces and jetted out of the gym. As soon as he pulled himself together, he called Raylina, gave her the version that Charlyn had given him, and told her to meet him at the hospital.

Since she was already at one of her usual hanging spots near Dudley Park, she was but a mere five-minute ride away, and when she arrived, she found that Royelle wasn't there, and Charlyn was asleep with her head buried in her crossed arms on Royelle's food tray table.

"Hi, Ms. Charlyn." Raylina softly greeted, tapping her lightly on her back.

"Oh. Hey Raylina." Charlyn whispered back as she raised her head. "Your brother got a hold of you, I see."

"Yes. Ma'am."

"It's been a while. How are you?" Charlyn asked, making small talk.

"I'm good. Where is she?" Raylina pointed to the empty space where

Royelle's bed should've been.

"They took her down for some testing. She should be back soon, honey."

"What happened to her?" She pulled up a chair sitting across from Charlyn.

"She's had a rough day, sweetie. Why don't we wait for your brother to get here so that I can tell y'all both at the same time? Is that ok?"

"That's fine. Did you call my father?"

"No. Royelle did not have him listed." Charlyn lied. "It was just you, Raymelle, and her friend Xandra."

"Does she know already?" Raylina asked.

"No. I thought it would be more appropriate for one of you to make that call."

"Ok."

Raylina walked out of the room, dialed out to Xandra, and the call went straight to voicemail. She tried a few more times and got the same result. After the last try, she finally gave up and left a voicemail.

"Hey, sis. It's Raylina. Royelle's in the hospital. We're at BMC. Call Raymelle or me when you get this."

As the two of them sat silently in the room, Raylina scrolled through her phone to see if Xandra was posting anything on her social media accounts, and it was dry. The last time she had posted it read, *"Death to niggas who ain't shit!"*

Since the majority of her past and present posts were negative in content when it came to scrams, her post didn't alarm much. It was her norm. However, the fact that she hadn't posted anything since then was concerning. That level of quiet was unusual for a social media whore like Xandra, who had Facebook, Instagram, Snapchat, Twitter, Tumblr, and was always on dating sites taunting people for shits and giggles. And although it was weird to see her social media accounts silent, Raylina's focus was on Royelle.

"Hey!" Raymelle said, hastily walking in the room smelling like a sweaty balls' locker room.

"Hey, Raymelle," Charlyn replied. Are you ok?" She asked.

"I'm a'ight. What's going on?."

Charlyn sighed before speaking.

"This is going to be a lot to take in, but Royelle got some bad news about Trevion."

"What's up with him? What the fuck did he do?" Raymelle questioned.

"He didn't do anything, Raymelle. Trevion passed away."

"What?! Nahhh!"

Instantly his eyes welled up with tears, and the room went silent as he and Raylina tried to process what Chalyn had just said.

"I'm sorry to tell you all like this. But there was no other way to say it."

"When?! How?!" He yelled, disregarding the fact that he was in the hospital.

"Apparently, a few days ago. The police said he was shhh…"

"Shot! Raymelle blurted out, cutting Charlyn off. "Nahhhhh, mannn! Shot!" He shouted in disbelief.

Raylina got up and closed the door to avoid any unwanted attention coming to the room.

"Raymelle. I know this is a lot, but please try to calm down for the sake of your sister."

He didn't say another word. He couldn't believe that Trevion, the dude he admired for so long, the one he knew would always protect his sister, keeping her out of harm's way, would be into any type of shit that would put him in the position to be murdered. Someone having it out for him to the point of murder just didn't seem legit. He was bracing himself for Charlyn to say that Royelle found out Trevion was cheating or doing something stupid with the business, causing her to go nuts. He never, not in a million years, thought that he'd have to prepare for news about Trevion being killed.

"But who would do something like that?" Raylina somberly asked.

As far as Charlyn was concerned, anyone was capable of murder if given the right opportunity and the right set of circumstances. And in his case, there was no telling. It could've been the so-called other wife, a business partner, a friend, anybody. It was too hard to tell and too early to speculate. But she did know that things were about to get very real in Royelle's life when she came out of this. She sat quietly for a moment deciding on how to punch them in the gut with the next and final blow. At this point, there was no option but to tell them. But before speaking, she remembered all the times Royelle told her about how immature and irresponsible her sister was and decided to wait to get Raymelle alone.

"What kinds of tests are they were running on her.?" Raylina asked.

"MRI's and CAT Scans to check for brain activity and internal bleeding, to make sure there's no damage anywhere that they can't see from the outside."

"Brain activity?! What's wrong with her brain? Are you saying she's brain dead?!"

Raylina's absentminded and overdramatic ass didn't hear shit Charlyn said.

"No. That's not what I'm saying. I know that when they took her, she was still unconscious. The test they run will tell them exactly what they need to know. Once the results come back, they'll be here to talk to y'all about it."

"This is crazy!" Raylina stormed out of the room to get some air.

As Raymelle turned to follow her, Charlyn grabbed him by his arm.

"Come here." She whispered, pulling him back.

"What's up?"

"Listen." Charlyn looked around as if being watched. "There is more to what added to her mental break."

"What's that?" His eyebrows frowned.

"When the detectives told Royelle that Trevion was killed, they told her his wife positively identified him."

"Wait?! What?!" Raymelle snapped back, keeping his voice down. "Wife? What wife?" You fucking bullshitting me right now, right? "

"No. Not at all. That's what they said."

"That shit can't be right. Are they sure?"

"They seemed pretty clear and confident about it."

"Nahhh bruh! That shit ain't sitting right."

He bit down on his balled-up fist, trying not to cause a scene or let anyone know that anger was flaming through his veins. When that method didn't seem to work, he put his hands on his head and turned in a small circle trying to cool down the hot lava that was rapidly flowing through him.

"I'm sorry I didn't say anything sooner, but I wanted to tell you in person, and I didn't want to be the one to tell Raylina. That's up to you and Royelle to decide."

"Nah. It's all good, Charlyn. I understand. So, what now? What the fuck is she supposed to do now?"

"I don't know. I'm going to try to locate where he's at and go from there."

"Aww man, this is fucked! My sister is about to completely lose her shit."

"She already has. That is why we're here, to begin with. So, all of us need to find a way to support her through this. It's about to be a long road ahead, Raymelle."

Raymelle couldn't believe that this was about to be their new norm with and for Royelle. He sat down in the chair, silent, no words, with emotionless expressions that spoke a thousand words. His thoughts were running rampant. It was hard enough for him to believe that Trevion was dead, and now this; another wife.

"Hello, everybody." The nurse greeted. "If you all wouldn't mind stepping out to the lobby for just a bit. We are going to get Mrs. Kingsley all situated, and we'll come back to get you when she's all set."

No one answered the nurse but did as they were told, moving in slow motion, trying to get a glimpse of what Royelle looked like. Her face was swollen, she was intubated, had IVs everywhere, a catheter, and all kinds of machines running. She had bruising, cuts to her face, dried up blood everywhere that the nurses tried their best to clean up, and her hair looked a hot mess. It definitely wasn't what they were expecting to see, and it saddened them all.

The look of worry and distress is what Charlyn saw on Raymelle's face. She would've paid a penny for his thoughts, but she was sure they shared the same feelings. Although for him, it was a bit different. That was his sister lying there unresponsive to everything going on around her, and there wasn't anything he could do to bring her out of it.

Raymelle stood in the waiting room with his back leaned against the wall and his head hanging low, engulfed in hurt. He closed his eyes and took a deep breath, reminiscing about his conversation with Trevion on the day he was set to marry Royelle.

"You ready, dawg?" Raymelle asked Trevion.

"You know it."

"I hope so. You know that's my sister, right?" His eyes darted into Trevion.

"Nigga yea. I've known for five years. What? We bout to have that brother-to-brother talk or some shit again?" Trevion laughed.

"Yea nigga. Again." Raymelle responded without a smile. *"That's my sister. I love her. I respect her. I'll do anything for her and will protect her at all costs. And that's what I'm telling you to do."*

"Man. I ain't hurt her since I've been with her. You know I love your sister, dawg. And I wouldn't waste my time or hers if I wasn't ready for this shit here." Trevion replied in an irritated tone.

"I feel you, dawg. I'm just reminding you." Raymelle responded.

"Sir." The nurse quietly repeated, breaking Raymelle's thoughts. "You can come back in now." She slightly smiled.

When Raymelle saw Royelle, brokenness covered his spirit. He was impaired by agony. The way Royelle looked made him feel like she was on her death bed. He stood silently, rubbing her left hand just starring. One could only assume what he was thinking as his facial expressions transitioned, with his thoughts shifting from sadness to anger. He tried not to cry, but that was his sister: the one who had it all, the one whose life was always under control and in order.

"Hello, everybody." Dr. Pisces said as she walked back into the room. "I am Dr. Pisces, and this is Dr. Schwartz, head of the Neurology team. Are you relatives of Mrs. Kingsley?"

"Yes. I'm her brother Raymelle, and that's our sister Raylina."

"Great. We wanted to talk to all of you about her current condition and discuss some recommendations. " Dr. Pisces said, turning it over to Dr. Schwartz.

"I'd like to start by saying that the test indicates no bleeding on the brain. That is a very good thing. While there is some slight swelling, her brain activity is ok right now. Currently, she's unconscious, essentially in a coma. How long that will last is up to her. It can be hours, days, weeks, or longer. We will be closely monitoring the activity the entire time she is here. As long as there are no major changes in activity, I don't see why she wouldn't come out of this. However, with every patient, nothing is the same. So, we will take this day by day."

"So why does she have this tube down her mouth and these straps on her?" Raylina asked.

"The tube is to help regulate her breathing." Dr. Pisces jumped in. "While she is in the coma, we want Royelle to rest and let the machine do all the work so that Royelle doesn't have to. As for the restraints, they are for everyone's safety, especially hers. When patients come out of a coma, most come out scared, alarmed, and sometimes combative because they do not know where they are or how they got here. We don't want her to cause harm to herself or harm to others. Additionally, we don't want her to pull that tube out of her mouth, causing any more damage to herself."

"So, what do we do from here? What happens next?" Raymelle asked.

"We will be moving her to the ICU as soon as a room becomes available. Visiting hours are open for ICU families, but overnight stays in the room are not permitted. However, I have seen some families camp out in the waiting room. You're welcome to do that at any time. We will be keeping a very close eye on her and her vitals and encourage you all to visit often, talk to her, play her favorite music, or whatever it is she likes. We believe that it helps stimulate the brain and helps them regain consciousness."

The Dr.'s understood it was a lot of information they had just given the family. So, they stopped talking and gave everyone a moment to pore over what they had just heard, but the silence in the room was so deafening you could hear a pin drop.

"Do you all have any more questions for Dr. Schwartz or me?" Dr. Pisces asked breaking up the silence.

Raymelle shook his head no, and Raylina stayed mute.

"Thank you, Dr.'s. I think that's all for now. If anything else comes up, I'll go find one of the nurses." Charlyn said.

"Our info and contacts are right there on the board behind you if you all need anything while you're down here. When she goes upstairs, she will have a board just like this one that will include the same information, on a daily basis and during shift change."

"Ok. Thank you." Charlyn shook their hands, and they walked out.

Dr.'s were good at picking up on cues from family members and knew when to shake a hand and when to walk away. Given the feel of the room, they knew it was best to leave Raymelle and Raylina alone with their sister to process the situation.

CHAPTER 6:
ALL ROADS CONNECT

*J*ayson was many things in the public eye. A man of great service, a homicide detective, respected pillar of his community, young, educated, professional, and well-established. But, behind closed doors, whenever sex was involved, he was anything but. His true-natured self with any woman always came to the surface.

He could've had any woman he wanted, but he was a bonified freak. And as a bachelor with no commitments to a soul and no children, he was free to do whatever he wanted with whomever. But most of the women he encountered were basic in bed. He wanted and needed more. So after going on several failed dates, he decided to reach out to various escort services looking for a particular type of girl.

Meeting Bella through Aruba's service was a godsend as far as he was concerned. He wasn't expecting a woman of her caliber to show up and show out, but she did. The fact that he was smitten by her was one thing, but her willingness to do anything that was demanded of her captured his interest even further. For dudes like Trevion and Jayson, Bella was the cream of the crop.

He walked into his room to Bella lying on her back with her legs wide open, finger fucking herself slowly. He silently stood back, listening to her moans, and watched her pleasing faces go from one extreme to the next. With each ooh and ahh, and the increase in the sounds of her gushiness expanding, his manhood grew more robust. When her breathing became progressively heavier, the speed of her hand increased its motion. And as the sounds of her moans became increasingly succulent, the more he couldn't wait to climb inside of her. But knowing she was getting closer to a climax, he didn't want to ruin the moment for her.

As he waited, he lubricated his hand with his saliva, wrapped it around his dick, and began stroking himself. And as she got closer and closer to her culmination, his strokes got faster and faster. The moment her body tensed up, followed by the loudest moan she had produced all night, he knew that was the it factor. He made his way over to the bed, pulled her closer to the edge towards him, put her feet on his shoulders, slid himself inside of her, closed his eyes, and began stroking her rapidly.

This was the type of shit that every nigga loved when they were with Bella. She had no restrictions. You paid, she played. She didn't give a damn about your profession, your race, your weight, your disability, or your gender. If the money fit the scale right, she was doing whoever, wherever, and whenever. As he continued stroking, his work phone started ringing. He glanced over while in mid-motion and noticed that it was a 781 area code. Immediately, Stoughton Police came to mind.

"Fuck! Hold up, Bella. I gotta take this. Might be work." He quickly pulled out and grabbed the phone.

"Aveen." He answered after the third ring.

"Ahh, yah. This is Detective Sean Rowley of the Stoughton Homicide unit returning your call.

"Oh yeah, yeah. Hold on just a second."

"I gotta take this. I'll be right back," he whispered to Bella and went into his study.

The phone was so loud that she and Shy could hear the call was from Stoughton Homicide, which piqued their interest given what had recently happened. The moment Jayson walked out, both girls jumped up and stood as close to the study as they could.

"Hey, Rowley. Sorry about that. Thanks for calling back, man."

"No sweat. What can I do for you?"

"Does the name Royelle Kingsley ring a bell?" Jayson asked.

Bella and Shy's eyes opened wide.

"No. But keep going."

"We interviewed her on a case that may or may not be related to yours. She mentioned that she provided you and your partner with some information into the Benton murder."

Rowley paused for a second to think about everyone he and Blackthorn had talked to in recent days.

"Ahhh yes! You're talking about the pretty Paralegal. I remember her. Yah, what's up? Is she in custody or something?"

"No. No. In the hospital. She was in a bad car accident."

Bella's eyes got even bigger. This was the first she had heard of Royelle being in the accident.

"No shit, huh?" Detective Rowley said.

"Yea. Not looking good last I checked."

"Ok. So, what can we help with?"

"I was hoping we could meet, cross reference some evidence, and see if we can't put two and two together. You know they say all roads connect, so there has to be some kind of connection between your murder and mines."

"Yah. I'll run it by my partner when he gets in, and we'll set something up."

"Great! I'll be expecting the call."

"Not a problem, brother. Anything we can do to help."

A few seconds before the call ended, both women jumped back in the bed and began to play with each other to avoid suspicion opf any kind.

"Well, what do we have here?" Jayson excitedly asked, walking in on Bella's ass in the air while she was face deep in Shy's pussy.

The sight of it all was so striking to him. He walked back over to them, grabbed Bella by the waist, and began fucking her from the back as if he had never stopped. He wanted to come so bad, but she was way too juicy, and it was way too soon.

To try and calm himself down, he laid on the bed and made Bella sit on his face while Shy sucked on him. Since it was his first time alighting upon Shy, he didn't know if she knew what to do or not; but he was sure she was nothing like Bella.

The entire time they were there, Shy played with herself and had to be directed on what to do next, and that, for Jayson, was a turnoff. They were all grown and knew what the assignment was, but she wanted to be taught, and Jayson wanted to fuck, plain and simple. As far as he was concerned, the only thing a bitch who didn't perform like Bella could do for him was calm his urges.

Once Bella came in his mouth, he ordered Shy onto her back, made Bella sit on her face, and he wasted no time tasting the nectars that projected from her Shy's insides. She was so sweet and juicy to him. And he was wildly impressed that she had the kind of clit that you could suck for hours, never knowing if it was swollen or not. It was huge, just like Bella's. He couldn't have missed it if he tried.

He started out sucking and finger fucking Shy roughly but noticed that he wasn't getting a response. It wasn't until he slowed down the pace with his finger and mouth motions that he began to feel her pussy pulsate and her secretions increase. And the more he did it in that manner, the more noticeable the changes in her body temperature became. Once he made her cum, he grabbed the lube for extra lubrication, squirted some on his right hand, and stroked it on his dick. He gently cocked her legs open and pushed them as far back as she could take it.

Unrevealed to Shy, dudes like Jayson prided themselves on making sure that whatever woman they were fucking at the time didn't get up unless she had an orgasm or squirted, no matter how long it took. A basic nut just wouldn't do. If his name was going to be attached to that later conversation he knew women had about men, then he needed to be sure it was *"gossiped"* about in the right way.

"Bella, grab her legs and don't let 'em go." He ordered.

Bella got off of Shy's face and knelt behind her. She grabbed Shy's legs, opened them, and slightly pulled them back. At this point, Shy knew there would be no escaping what Jayson was about to do.

"Oh naw! You good little mama. Too late now." Jayson said when she reached her hand out to try and stop him.

By the time Jayson was done talking, his almost nine-inch dick was completely inside of her. Her body was so tense, but it wasn't going to stop him from stroking. In fact, it was a turn-on for him, knowing that she was not only afraid of the size and thickness of his log but also how he was about to penetrate her pearl hole. But the more shit he talked while stroking, the easier it became for Shy to tolerate his length and fatness. His voice and direction had become much more tantalizing, making it easier for her to only focus on the pleasure, not pain.

As he listened to the loud moans of both women in the air, he looked at Bella and said, "You're next."

"I've been waiting." She replied.

Hearing Bella's response excited him so deeply it made him stroke Shy faster and harder until he noticed she was about to cum.

"Back up, Bella." He ordered.

Bella released Shy's legs and moved to the side, allowing Jayson room to get in deeper.

"Cum for me bitch!" He ordered while stroking harder. "I said cum for me bitch!" He fucked harder and faster.

He knew it was coming. He could feel it. As soon as he gently touched her clit, Shy let out a yelping scream, and her body shook uncontrollably. She had orgasmed like she never had in all her years of fucking and breaking up happy homes. Once she completely released herself, he pulled out and looked down at himself, excited to see her cum all over him. He was pleased with his accomplishment. He quickly pushed her to the side like she wasn't shit and gunned for Bella.

"Come 'er you."

He grabbed Bella by the face and exchanged a sloppy French kiss with her before grabbing the washcloth to clean himself off. He turned her around, grabbed the lube, and squeezed it all over her ass. He loved the sight of seeing it shiny or wet. He lubed himself again and slid right in—no barriers, no push back, no hesitation, no problems. Easy money.

"Play with ya pussy hoe!" He demanded.

Bella did as she was told, and he began fucking her as if it would be the last time they'd meet.

"Fuck that ass, daddy!" Bella hollered.

"Bitch! Don't talk to me like that!" He said, pulling her hair.

"Fuck that ass detective!" She said louder.

Bella knew all she had to do was use her ability to talk shit, and she had him. His weaknesses weren't hard to learn, and she used them against him each and every time they met. Once his moans got louder and his strokes faster, stronger, and deeper, she knew she had him. It was just a matter of seconds now.

"Bust that ass open, Mr. Officer!" She yelled.

"Oh, shit bitch! You playing!"

He grabbed her ass cheeks tighter and did just as he was told. He fucked and fucked and fucked her, and not once did she budge no matter how hard he went in. When he noticed how wet she was, dripping onto the bed, it made him fuck her even harder.

"Shitttt!' He yelled as he touched her.

"You like that shit detective, don't you?" She said in a sexy voice. "Fuck me harder, and it gets wetter." She kept the same tone.

Her ass was so good to him he couldn't even respond. The only thing he could do was stroke and enjoy the sensation that was subduing him.

"Fuck you waiting for detective?! Fuck that ass, bust it open, and cum in that muthafucker for me!" She teased and hollered some more.

Soon as the words released from her lips, it was over for Jayson. He came so hard and fast that his knees quickly buckled, causing him to lose his balance while he was still inside of her. She looked over at Shy and mouthed for her to get dressed. And since she didn't want to fuck anything up, she stayed in her face-down ass-up position until he was ready to pull out.

"You good?" She asked when he finally slid out and laid on his back.

"Yea. I'm goooddd. "He chuckled, breathing heavily in the process.

Bella smiled, grabbed her stuff, went into the master bathroom, quickly washed up, and got dressed.

"We gotta get going." She said, walking back into the room. "But you got my number. Anytime, any place, any day, any number of girls, you just ring my line. Ok, daddy?"

"I got you. But aye. You never did tell me her name."

Bella looked over at Shy and saw the subservient look on her face.

"Shy. Her name is Shy."

"I can see why." He shot back. "Money's where it's always at."

"Ok, baby." Bella blew Jayson a kiss, grabbed the money off the mantel, and both ladies walked out.

"Why didn't you just tell him my real name?"

"For the same reason, he doesn't know mine. Now shut the fuck up, McKenzie, and come on."

CHAPTER 7:
SURPRISE, SURPRISE!

When detective Rowley told Jayson he'd get back to him, three days later was not the turnaround time Detective Aveen anticipated. He understood, though. Sometimes there were things on the job that took precedent over others. So, when he got the text to meet Rowley at the Stoughton Police Department, he was eager and wasted no time making his way. He contemplated on whether or not to bring his partner Detective Presley but decided against it. Presley had a way of pissing people off with his know-it-all attitude, and right now, that was the last thing or impression that Jayson wanted to leave with S.P.D.

As soon as Jayson pulled up to the station, he was shocked to see that the setup was different for a suburban town. It was smack dab in the center of a residential neighborhood instead of tucked away in the cut somewhere. Police stations like Stoughton's were only seen in the hoods of Boston, like Dudley Square, Fields corner, Jamaica Plain, or even Head Quarters, which sits in front of the Mission Hill projects and not too far from the Lenox Street one, which was right up the street. Given its location and exterior appearance, he was taken aback the moment he entered the station and saw it was nothing like his. Everything appeared to be updated, and it smelled much cleaner too. It may have been in a residential area, but it had a suburban air and cleanness to it.

"Can I help you, sir?" The female desk cop asked.

"Yes. Detective Aveen here to see Detective Rowley." He handed her his ID and badge number for her record-keeping log.

"All set, sir. Detective Rowley will be down momentarily." She handed him back his belongings.

The longer he waited and looked around, the more he realized that the Milton Police Department was the great-grandfather of all police stations. They weren't up to date on shit, and it was sad. It just proved their Roman Times way of thinking. It's hard to get fresh ideas with old mentalities, and that's all Milton Police housed; old people with old mentalities.

"Detective Aveen?" Rowley called out, approaching Jayson.

"Rowley?" Jayson questioned unsure if that was him.

"Sean. Call me Sean." He stuck his hand out to shake Jayson's.

"A'ight Sean. Jayson. Thanks for meeting with me."

"No problem. Sorry it took so long. Follow me."

Jayson followed Sean's lead up the stairs to the second floor. When Sean badged in, Jayson was wowed at how different their setup was compared to the one at Milton P.D. The open office space was wide, housing ten homicide detectives, each with their own high paneling cubicle shaped like the letter H for privacy. He hated to admit it, but he was feeling a little salty that his station looked like a version out of Law and Order, where it was just a desk, a phone, and police everywhere, being loud, obnoxious, and trying to work amongst the insanity.

"Everybody, this is Detective Jayson Aveen. Jayson, these are all the Bobbies of this unit."

"All the what?" Jayson chuckled.

"It's cops in British," Sean replied.

"Yea, some shit he ain't! He wishes he was British!" Detective Blackthorn laughed, getting up out of his seat.

"That's my asshole partner Detective Thomas Blackthorn."

"Hey! How are yah?" Thomas said.

"I'm good, thanks." Jayson extended his hand to shake Thomas's.

"We're going this way," Sean said as the three of them walked towards the conference room, each with folders in their hands.

"So, what can we help you with, Jayson?" Thomas jumped right to it as they took their seats.

"It's my understanding that you all are investigating the murder of Gail Benton and have interviewed her neighbor Royelle Kingsley," Jayson said.

"Yah. That's true." Thomas responded as they took their seats.

"Well, her husband, or should I say boyfriend, has been murdered."

Jayson pulled out the photos from the crime scene and slid them across the table, looking on as Sean and Thomas analyzed them. They couldn't believe that the person they were hoping was good for Mrs. Benton's murder was now a murder victim himself.

"When did this shit fucking happen?" Sean asked, looking up from the photos.

"According to forensics, it's been about a week, give or take.."

"So, this wasn't too soon after our victim was killed. Fuckkk!" Sean shouted.

By all accounts, all the evidence they had so far pointed at Trevion as being the likely suspect for Brenton's murder, but it still wasn't enough to call him the murderer definitively. They never had the opportunity to pick him up and put him in the hot seat for questioning. And now, the potential for having Benton's murder solved was slim to none, not to mention, closure for the family was also highly unlikely.

"So." Thomas started again. "How does your case tie into this one?" He asked.

"I'm not sure yet. I was hoping to learn more about the information Royelle shared concerning the Benton murder. Maybe something she said or didn't say would help with this one."

"You guys think she's somehow involved in both murders?" Sean questioned.

"Not sure yet. That's why I'm here. She doesn't seem like the type, but you never know."

"Let me get in touch with our video analyst Zack and see if he has anything for us yet. Then, we can view it all together."

Sean called down to Zack while Jayson and Thomas talked about insignificant things just to pass the time, and not more than a few minutes later, Zack was upstairs with items in hand.

"Good Afternoon Queens!" Zack hollered, walking through the door.

"Zack! Cut the bullshit." Sean snapped, walking back towards his desk with Jayson and Thomas.

"Oh! So, I take it you don't wanna see what I got for you then, huh?" Zack pointed at the collection of items in his hand, turned around, and started walking back towards the exit sign.

"This shit better be good, Zack!" Sean said.

Sean's attitude straightened right up. It's what he had been waiting for. Anything that could help him bring Mrs. Benton's case to a close was a win.

"Mmm Hmmm! That's what I thought." Zack giggled. "Who's your friend?" Zack looked Jayson up and down.

"This is Detective Aveen from Milton."

"Nice to meet you, sir," Zack said with spice in his eyes.

"Hurry the hell up, prick! Show us what you got." Sean slapped Zack upside his head.

Zack laughed as he sat down at Sean's desk. He inserted the USB into the computer and waited for Mrs. Benton's videos to load as the other detectives gathered around him.

"So, it took us a little while to comb through everything, but who's the man?!" Zack chuckled. "The reports of Mrs. Benton being a stalking bitch, serves her right. That lady was meticulous in keeping videos of everything. And I mean everything! It took days to comb through all of this shit. The damn lady even recorded the strays screwing, for heaven's sake. But as they say, cameras talk, and they don't lie when they do."

"Zack!" Sean hollered. "Get to the damn point, man!"

"Ok, ok! Calm your tits, friend." Zack rolled his eyes. "Most of it is nothing, just a quiet suburban neighborhood that became quite interesting within the last week or so."

"How so?" Sean asked.

"Hold on there, Princess."

Zack finally got the video cued up to where he needed it and began to run it. Sean and some of the other detectives who had gathered around Zack all listened and watched closely as he pointed out the woman who was constantly caught on tape creeping through Royelle's backyard and into her backdoor.

"Who's that? Were you able to get a read on the plate?" Sean asked.

"Not exactly. It has a dark-tinted plate cover over it. And she never comes during the day."

"Ok. So, what's so interesting about her? It doesn't look like she's breaking any laws?"

"Well, she's not, buttt...

"Zack!"

Zack looked back at Sean. " Did my sister give you any last night? Because you sure are being snippy today, friend. I'm the gay one here, and you're acting more girly than me."

The other detectives laughed.

"Fuck you! Get to the point, man. Time is money, and you always take thirty minutes to tell a three-minute story."

"Calm the fuck down, Rowley. Let the man work." One of the other detectives said.

Sean stuck his middle finger up at him.

"So, what I was trying to say before I was rudely interrupted by my brother-in-law," Zack pulled his short hair behind his right ear, rolling his eyes at Sean. " The man standing in that doorway," he pointed at Trevion, "is having an affair. Do you see the time-lapse from the time she arrives versus the time she leaves? I'm sure she's not there for milk and cookies. Not to mention their saliva exchange right before she leaves.

Jayson looked at the video with his blood boiling when he saw all the footage of Bella and Trevion tongue kissing every time she came in and out of his house. But he couldn't say shit and had to stay mindful of his facial expressions. How would he even begin to explain that he was fucking the neighborhood hoe if someone ever found out about their connection? The plot had just gotten thicker, and he needed to reach out to Bella now more than ever.

"How much you wanna bet his wife doesn't know what the cameras do. What if —" Zack continued.

"Mrs. Benton put two and two together and was gonna say or did say something." Sean interrupted.

"Bingo! Bango! Now you're getting it, sweetheart. But that's not it." Zack fast-forwarded the tape a bit. "You see this car. Whoever this is, has been circling the block, all hours of the night like their casing the neighborhood."

"Can't see a plate for shit on this car either," Sean said, looking a bit closer at the screen, trying to catch a better glimpse of the plate number.

"Yah, I know. You can thank the night air and shitty cameras for that." Zack said.

"So, given what's on these tapes, would you say Trevion, rather than Royelle, would be a more appropriate fit for Benton?" Jayson asked after viewing the tapes.

"Remains to be seen. Everybody's a suspect until they're not." Sean replied. "On the surface, it does look like Trevion is good for Benton's murder, and I hate that it does cause I wanted to see that bastard rot in hell for what he did to that lady and those dogs." Sean continued.

"Hmm. But it looks like somebody put Trevion through hell when they killed him, so I guess you got your wish in a sense." Jayson patted Sean on the shoulder.

"Maybe. But I like said, everybody, is a suspect until they aren't."

"Yea. You're right about that. Thanks for meeting me, gentleman. I think I have what I need for now. Sean, do you think I can get some still shots of some of these video images?" Jayson asked.

"Yah. That shouldn't be a problem. Zack, can you get those for him?"

"It won't take but a minute." Zack smiled at Jayson.

By the time they went to the conference room to get Jayson's things and walk back towards Sean's desk, Zack was already approaching them with a manila file in hand. It was the quickest thing Zack had accomplished to date.

"Here's what you requested. Anything else you gentleman need?" Zack smiled at Jayson again.

"That'll be all." Sean snatched the file and sent him on his way. "Here you go, man, and good luck with your case. If there's anything, anything at all, that I can help with, call me."

"You got it, Sean. Thanks for your help. Later Blackthorn!" Jayson yelled across the hall.

"Ah! Fuck him!" Sean laughed. He shook Jayson's hand, and they both agreed to stay in touch for the sake of the cases.

Jayson rushed back to his car and immediately called Bella.

"Heyyy Detective." She seductively answered.

"Bella! We need to talk."

"Are you ok?"

"Where are you?" He ignored her question.

"I'm around."

"Meet me at the park behind Houghton's Pond in twenty minutes."

"Ummm, ok. Do I need to—

Before she could finish her sentence, Jayson hung up the phone.

CHAPTER 8:
THE STREETS NEVER SLEEP

Twenty-six minutes after Jayson hung up with Bella, he pulled up to the park to find her already standing outside, leaned up in a sexy position on the hood of her car. She smiled as he pulled into his space and quickly noticed the gesture wasn't returned.

"What's going on, Detective? Are you ok?" She asked as he stepped out of his Black Charger.

"Hmph. I don't know. You tell me."

"Tell you what?" Bella had a surprised look upon her face.

"I didn't know you were seeing potential murder suspects as clients."

"Wha—what do you mean?" Her words quivered.

"Bella, don't play stupid with me." He snapped.

"Ok, Jayson." Bella stood up straight. "I don't know what you're talking about. You called me all the way over here to talk about some damn clients."

"No! Not some damn clients!"

Jayson turned around, walked back to his car, reached through the rolled-down window, and grabbed Trevion's file.

"I'm talking about this damn client!" He threw the file on the hood of her car.

When she opened it, her mouth dropped. She tried to maintain her composure, but it was too late; her initial response said it all.

"Uh-huh. I thought you'd react like that. So, what's up? I need to know everything you know about him and his wife, and I mean now!" He hollered.

Bella was marveled. She stared in disbelief as she looked at the pictures of her creeping through the yard, coming in and out of the house, and exchanging kisses with Trevion. She couldn't fathom the idea that the entire time she was sneaking around, she was also being clocked.

"Say something!" Jayson hollered.

Bella jumped at the sound of his voice.

"What do you want me to say?" She nervously asked.

"How long you been fucking him, Bella?"

"I don't know!"

"The truth Bella! How long?!"

"I don't knowwww!" She hollered back. "It's been a long time."

"Where were you the night he was killed?"

"I was in New York. Here! I can show you."

Bella went into her car's glove compartment, pulled out the receipts from all the tolls she incurred on the drive down, and the receipt from the Marriott Hotel she stayed at on Broadway.

"This don't mean shit!" He yelled, looking down at the receipts she handed to him.

"Oh, it doesn't!"

Bella opened her phone and began showing him all the pictures she took from inside the Marriott and while in Times Square with the time and date stamp from the same weekend Trevion was murdered.

"I wasn't fucking here when he was killed! I didn't fucking do it and don't have shit to do with it! I heard how that man fucking died. Shame on you for thinking I could ever do something like that. And how come no one else has come to question me about it yet?"

Jayson took an intense breath.

"Bella. Do you have a record? Any priors whatsoever?"

"No."

"Any fingerprints on file?"

"No."

"Be lucky that the picture quality ain't shit! It makes it hard for anyone to identify you."

"Well, you knew it was me."

"Yea. Cause I know you and your car." He pointed at the car in the picture.

"So now what am I supposed to do?"

"Man, just lay low. If they want you for questioning, they'll come looking for you."

"Jayson, why do you keep saying they? Who the fuck are they? Ain't you handling the case?

"They? They are the Stoughton Police. I'm handling his murder. They're handling the Benton one. These pictures we're originally only connected to her murder, but now we can use them for his."

"Oh! Uh-uh! I didn't do either of those muthafuckas! Ain't nobody fin to pin shit on me!"

"Well, if you didn't do it, you don't have shit to worry about then... do you?" Jayson said nonchalantly.

Bella looked over at him and rolled her eyes.

"Jayson, you know me. You know I wouldn't do this. I do what I do in the bed, and that's that. I'm not built for murder." She cried. "And I never had a problem with that man. He paid faithfully like everyone else I've ever encountered—"

"Stop! I don't wanna hear shit else! You said you didn't do it, and you weren't here. Leave it at that. But you know, like I know, the streets never sleep. And now that I know you're connected to the case, we can't see each other anymore."

Jayson grabbed the file from the hood of her car and walked back to his own.

"Jayson, wait!" Bella hollered.

He didn't turn back. He jumped in his ride and peeled off.

"Fuckkkk!" Bella yelled.

She jumped in her car and whipped out of the parking lot, hauling ass down 93 North, weaving in and out of traffic.

"Awww fuck! Come onnn!" She hollered when she saw all the red taillights meeting at the congested split coming from 24.

She was a nervous wreck. What Jayson had on her was very telling, and while she may have been fucking him, it was always strictly business. He owed her no loyalty. The fact that he even came to her with it on the low shocked the shit out of her, especially knowing that he had a career to maintain and an image to uphold.

"Fuck this!" She said.

Seeing the standstill traffic ahead of her, she decided to hop off at exit 2A, Milton. Once she got off the highway, going through Milton was easy. The traffic was light, and the traffic lights were all on go mode. You catch one; you catch em' all. As she got closer to the spot where it was rumored Trevion had been killed, she took a deep breath and sighed. It was the first time since he died that she had been in that area, and it didn't feel good. She swallowed the knot in her throat and drove a bit faster in an attempt to get as far away from that area as possible.

Soon as she was out of Milton and into the hoods of Dorchester, she started taking every cut, corner, and side street she could think of, just to avoid the annoying hood traffic. When she finally pulled up to the Old Colony housing projects, the same usual niggas that sat on the stoop were the same niggas that Xandra saw sitting there a few weeks prior, doing the same lame shit; nothing. Bella parked her car, grabbed her shit, and sprinted across the street to the building as if she was being chased.

"What's up, little mama?" The dude on the bottom step asked.

"Hey, y'all!" She hastily responded.

"You a'ight shorty?" They clowned, noticing her worried body language.

"I'm good." She lied.

They opened up enough space for her to get by, and she ran up every flight of stairs until she reached apartment D1 on the fourth floor. Before she could get her breathing regulated or her fist balled up to knock, Aruba opened the door.

"Well, how fucking long were you planning on staying out here?" She joked.

Bella cracked a small smile.

"I was coming. I just had to catch my breath."

"Ok. Well, you good now?" Aruba asked.

"Barely," Bella said, still trying to catch her breath, wondering how Aruba even knew she was there.

"Fuck you running up the stairs for anyway. You coulda walked, you know." Aruba laughed as she walked into the kitchen to grab the Patron margaritas she had just made.

"Here you go." She passed Bella a drink. "So, what got you on edge today?"

Bella guzzled her first drink, got up, and poured herself another one before speaking.

"Ok. Do you remember the client I went to go see a few days ago?"

"Which one, Bella? You got a shit load of them."

"The one me and McKenzie went to go see."

"Yea, ok. Now you got my attention. What about him?"

"I met with him before coming here, and he got evidence —"

"Evidence?! Evidence of what?!" Aruba's voice quickly elevated.

Bella tensed up. She knew what she was getting ready to say was about to cause a serious problem. She took another gulp of her drink and then spoke.

"Evidence of me coming in and out of Trevion's house."

Before Bella could say or do anything else, Aruba had slapped her so hard, it caused her drink to drop onto the carpeted floor.

"You stupid bitch! How many times did I tell you not to go over there?! How many?! What the fuck was you over there for anyway?!"

"How was I supposed to know the house was being watched?" Bella snapped back.

"That's beside the fucking point! And I asked you a muthafucking question! What the fuck were you doing over there?!"

A deadly stillness protruded from Bella as she starred at Aruba. She was shocked by the slap and wanted so badly to beat Aruba's ass, but she knew better and knew her position.

"What?! You wanna do something? You feeling tough or some shit?!"

Aruba met Bella at eye level. "You fucked up. Not me, you! Not following the fucking rules puts all of us in a fucked up position. How much does he fucking know about McKenzie?" Aruba stood back up.

"Nothing."

"Not even her name?!" Aruba yelled.

"No. He thinks her name is Shy."

"So, what exactly did he say, Belle?!"

"Not much. He asked how I was connected to Trevion and told me that he's not investigating the case; Stoughton is."

"Stoughton?! Why Stoughton?!"

"Because the tapes are connected to the murder of Trevion's neighbor. So basically, I can be questioned on both."

"Awww, man Belle! This shit just keeps on getting better, doesn't it?!. You fucked up royally!"

Bella kept her head down, not saying a word.

"I'm gonna have to do some serious damage control. In the meantime, play everything cool. Don't say shit to McKenzie; don't even bring her on another job. It's too fucking risky right now."

Aruba guzzled her drink, walked back to the kitchen, and poured herself two shots of Patron. There was no room for error, and having Bella on tape was the worst mistake any of them could have made.

CHAPTER 9:
THE DEPARTED

ood morning Mrs. Adala." Suzanne greeted as she did every shift. "Today, the sun is out, it's shining beautifully, the birds are chirping, the grass is much greener than I have seen it in quite some time, and it looks like God has the clouds opening up. It almost looks like he's making a pathway for something; you oughta see this. You'd love it." She rambled on as she opened the blinds and curtains. She talked so much, looking in the other direction that she never noticed Adala's Olive skin looking rather chaffed and pale. It wasn't until she got closer to her bedside that she saw the obvious.

"Mrs. Adala?" The cracking in her voice deepened.

She touched her hand, and Adala was still warm like a Summer's day. But, to be 100% sure of what she suspected, she checked for a pulse.

"Ohhh no! Mrs. Adala." She heavily sighed.

She sat on the edge of the bed and began crying for a few reasons. One, she loved Adala very much. Even though attachment was something medical personnel were trained not to have with their patients, Adala was the one that she thrived on coming to work for. Two, she knew the profound love Royelle had for her mother, and Suzanne's inability to notify Royelle of her mother's passing was devastating.

"If there's one thing I know about you, it's that you were a god-fearing woman. And there's no doubt in my mind that the pathway I see in the sky was made especially for you." Suzanne said.

She let her tears fall for as long as she could, then pulled herself together and said a prayer over Adala. She gently covered her up, exposing only her face, and kissed her on her forehead before walking back out towards the nurse's station.

When nurse Mikino saw Suzanne with her head hanging low and her shoulders sagging, immediately, she knew what time it was. Mikino gave Suzanne a tight hug, and the other nurses joined in, tightening the circle. They knew how she felt about Adala and the Blevins family; blood couldn't have made them any closer.

"Listen. Go to the lounge and take a minute. Whatever you haven't done yet, we will finish." Mikino spoke as she released her grip.

"Thank you, Mikino, but I have to be the one to make the call to the family."

"Ok. That's fine. You handle that, and we will do the rest."

Suzanne thanked Mikino, grabbed Adala's file, and walked to the conference room to make the call in private. She sat down on the Black mesh executive office chair and exhaled. She always hated this part of her job. The long sighs and sometimes the screams of loved ones seemed to never stop ringing in her ears. But, none of the death notifications she's made in the past were as daunting as the one she was about to make. This time was different; it reminded her so much of the time she had to call her siblings about her own mother's passing. The anxiety she felt and how her body tensed up from the grief was all too familiar.

She lowered her head, folded her hands on top of the Oval, Cherry Wood table, and prayed out loud, asking God to guide her words and strengthen the family as they were about to be hit with yet another blow. The idea of calling Rayford nauseated her. She hated that he was granted Power of Attorney shortly after Royelle was in the coma. Be that as it may, he was the first point of contact, and she had to follow protocol regardless of her feelings towards him. She picked up the receiver dreading to make the call. Being that it was barely seven in the morning, she prayed he wouldn't answer, and as soon as the call went to voicemail, she sighed a breath of relief and left a voicemail.

"Good day. This is Angel Zone calling. Please call us back as soon as possible. Thank you."

Knowing what she knew about Royelle's situation, she was certain notifying Raymelle would send him into a frenzy, but she was left with no other choice, and frankly, it was her preferred choice over Rayford. Raymelle dealt with a full deck of cards, unlike his father. The phone rang and rang before it went to voicemail. She hung up and called right back.

"Hello?" He answered on the third ring with a croaky voice.

"Raymelle?"

"Yea. Who's this?"

The number was unfamiliar to him, and in normal circumstances, he wouldn't have even bothered picking it up that early in the morning. But given everything that was going on in his family, anything was possible.

"It's Suzanne."

"Oh, hey." He quickly sat up, clearing his throat. "What's going on? Mom's good?"

She could hear the worry and anxiety in his voice.

"Well, that's what I'm calling you about, Raymelle. She—"

"Awww, man! Come on, man! Don't tell me that. I'm on my way!"

Suzanne didn't need to say anything else. Raymelle felt the devastation in his bones. He hopped out of bed with only his boxers on, grabbed the clothes he had on the night before, and bolted to the bathroom, screaming Raylina's name throughout their small two-bedroom apartment. With her room being right next to the bathroom, it was hard for her to ignore the yelling.

"Brooo. Why are you yelling?" She wiped the sleep out of her eyes while standing in her doorway.

"Get dressed! We gotta get to momma!" He mumbled with a mouthful of toothpaste.

"What?" Raylina frowned.

He quickly rinsed his mouth out.

"I said get dressed! It's momma!"

Her eyes widened. She quickly turned around, threw on her beauty supply slides and a hoodie over her one-piece footless pajama. She grabbed her travel-size mouth kit off the dresser and paid no attention to her messy hair.

"You gonna brush your teeth?" Raymelle asked.

She raised her hand to show him her kit. "There's no time. I'll handle it over there."

Raylina had no idea what was happening with her mother, and her being gone was the furthest thing from her mind. She wanted to ask Raymelle what was going on but could tell that he was in no mood to answer questions from the way he was driving. She made sure her seatbelt was secured and stayed quiet as he continued to move at lightning bolt speed, weaving through inner-city traffic, running every red light in his path.

Knowing how painful the situation would be for Adala's family, Suzanne went back to Adala's room to get her ready, only to find that Mikino and the team of nurses left no stone unturned. While the chaplain was on his knees praying over Adala, Suzanne starred with tears streaming down her face. She couldn't believe how paradisical Adala looked.

Everyone at Angel Zone knew about Royelle's desire to see her mother looking nothing less than ambrosial when it was her time, and they did not fail to deliver. She laid peacefully in the White Vintage gown and ballerina slippers that Royelle brought her for this moment alone. Her hair was neatly brushed, adorned with a White flower headpiece, and the light makeup was an attempt to disguise her slight discoloration.

The smell from the well-rounded floral aroma of Adala's Monique Lhuillier perfume filled the air. The blinds were closed, and one White candle stayed lit on her dresser. Overall, the room had a serene feel to it. It was such a calming feel and sight for Suzanne that she hoped the same feeling would attach itself to Adala's family when they arrived.

"Suzanne." The chaplain said as he rose to his feet.

"Good Morning, Father."

"And a glorious morning it is, my daughter. Have you made contact with the family?"

"Yes. They are en route." She looked over at Adala.

"You know that to be absent from the body is to be present with the Lord, don't you?"

"Yes. It's just —"

"Daughter." He interrupted. "Those morning skies opened up for her today. Did you see it?" He smiled.

Suzanne was shocked to hear him say exactly what she had been thinking and feeling all along.

"God always welcomes the departed with open arms. Always. The open sky is proof of that. If there is anything to take away from this, it is that she went peacefully. She looks peaceful, and therefore, peace is what she would expect from those who loved and cared for her, including you."

"Thank you, Father." Suzanne lightly smiled. " May I have a moment with her?"

"As you wish. In the name of the Father, the Son, and the Holy Spirit. Amen."

He did the four-point cross symbol from forehead to chest, shoulder to shoulder, walked towards the door, and stopped short in front of Suzanne.

"Daughter, death comes for us all. Do not weep for her. Be glad that she is rejoicing with our Lord and Savior, the same one she loved and worshipped so much."

He lightly tapped Suzanne on her shoulder and walked out of the room.

CHAPTER 10:
SUZANNE

*R*aylina, still unaware of what was happening, followed Raymelle's footsteps closely as they rushed through the double doors at Angel Zone and right past the reception area. Neither of them cared about the sign-in sheet that was required for visitors to sign. The only focus was making it to Adala's room where Suzanne was, and as soon as Raymelle opened her door, he lost it.

"Ahhh, man! Nahh!" He hollered.

He threw his back up against the wall and slid down to the floor, covering his face as he sobbed.

"Momma?" Raylina's voice cracked. "Momma?" She repeated, walking closer to her. "Momma?" She touched her hand. "Please, momma! No! Please! Wake up, Momma!"

Her pleas were that of a daughter who simply didn't believe what had happened. She wanted her to wake up, reach back out for her hand, move her head towards her voice, something, anything, to make the pain she was feeling go away. There was nothing. Suzanne stayed lulled and allowed them to process everything in the way they needed to. However, it pierced her heart to see Raymelle's pain and listen to Raylina's implorations, but she had to put her pain aside so that she could comfort them through theirs.

"Raymelle." She squatted down to his level.

Through all the anguish he was experiencing, he slowly lifted his head and opened his eyes.

"I am deeply sorry for your loss. Truly I am. I'm going to give you and your sister some time, but I'll be right out here at the nurse's station whenever you need me. Ok?"

He nodded his head, and Suzanne walked out of the room softly, closing the door behind her.

"How are they, Suzanne?" Mikino asked when she returned to the desk.

"As good as can be expected." She sat down and kept watch of Adala's room door to open.

"Raymelleee…What about Royelle?" Raylina sobbed.

"I know, sis. I know."

He stood to his feet, walked over, and grabbed his sister, hugging her tightly. They were both saturated with sadness and grief, but of the two of them, Raymelle knew the burden of responsibility fell on him.

"Lina, stay here with momma. you gonna be a'ight for a second?"

She vaguely nodded.

" Are you sure?"

He needed the reassurance that she could handle being by herself with their now-deceased mother. When she nodded again, he stepped out into the hallway to call Rayford, but each call went straight to voicemail.

"You gotta be fucking shitting me." He gritted his teeth.

His mind scrambled, and his thoughts did not come easy as he contemplated on who else he could call. He barely knew any of their family living in Germany; therefore, he didn't bother with them and calling his Jamaican side was a no-go too. There wasn't shit either side would be able to help with anyway.

Like loose ink on paper, his stress levels were rampantly spreading. His sad emotions were slowly turning into anger as his heart pounded hard against his ribcage. '*None of this is supposed to be happening,*' he thought. And yet, here he was dealing with two of the worst things he had ever had to face.

To avoid his wrath from engulfing him in the one place that has been nothing but good to his entire family, he took a moment to slow his anger by inhaling and exhaling long, steady breaths. The more breaths he took, the further out his frenzy pushed away. It allowed space for his muddled mind to become unclouded and gain him some clarity. And just like that, Charlyn came to mind. He shuffled through his contact list until he came across *"Sis's Boss."*

"Hello. Good Morning, Raymelle." She immediately answered.

"Hey, Charlyn. We need your help." He said in a low voice.

"Of course. Of course. What's going on with Royelle?" She assumed.

"It's not Royelle. It's —"

"Your mother?" She interrupted in a sad tone. She didn't know how she knew; she just knew.

"Mannn." His tears started again.

Charlyn could hear the despair and bleakness Raymelle was facing through the phone's airwaves.

"Raymelle. I am so sorry." She lowed. "I'm on my way. Don't do anything until I get there."

He breathed a sigh of relief. It was like every block he was carrying had crumbled all at once. He knew Charlyn was all about business and would do everything possible to help get things on track.

"Suzanne." Dr. Patel called out, breaking her focus. "Can I see you for a moment?"

They both walked to his office, where Charge Nurse Beverly, and Program Director, Nicole, were already seated. Immediately an uncomfortable feeling subdued her. She felt like she had just walked into an ambush. With a profound look on her face, she took a seat in the last empty chair.

"Don't look so crazy, Suzanne. You're not in any kind of trouble." Nicole said.

"I never thought I was. People who don't do their jobs are the ones most concerned. I didn't know there was a meeting going on, is all." She snapped back.

Nicole pressed her lips in agitation and looked back over towards the doctor. Suzanne didn't care. She was not in the mood for Nicole or her bullshit. They already had a strained relationship, and every time Nicole tried to fix it, she attempted it at the most inopportune time with the most inappropriate comments or jokes.

"The reason we called you in here, for starters, was to check on your mental and emotional status." Dr. Patel said.

"I'm fine, Dr. Of course, I'm saddened by her passing as I would be for any of our patients. But I'm ok."

"We understand, and we're glad to know that. As with any of the departed, we want to be sure that our staff —"

"Doctor." Suzanne disrupted. "I'm ok. I don't need to go home. I don't need a minute. My goal now is to ensure her family has all that we can offer within our limits."

"Wonderful! Well, now that we have that established, we wanted to inform you that we'll have to move Mrs. Blevins soon."

Suzanne's eyes widened. "Sir. She just passed away within the last four or five hours, and her family has been here all of thirty minutes." Suzanne responded in an irritated tone.

"We understand, Suzanne. But we have a protocol we must follow." Nicole chipped in.

"Protocol?"

"Yes, Suzanne. But aside from that, you know, on average, rigor mortis starts to set in between 2-4 hours after death. Therefore, we need to get in touch with the morgue to coordinate a time for pick up. Also, we need maintenance to tidy up the room for the next live-in."

"Hmph. I see." Suzanne, visibly upset at this point, sat straight up. "This meeting is really about the money. Sure, a small piece of it may be about the transfer, but, if we can be honest, we've had patients deceased in their room for more than six hours for one reason or another. But, I guess as long as she stays in that room, the more money you lose, right? I mean, it's impossible to charge a daily rate for a dead person, isn't it?"

"Suzanne. It's far more than that." Nicole said.

"Nicole, with all due respect, It's only that, and I can't be convinced otherwise. However, I will speak with the family and advise them of this."

Suzanne snapped back.

If Nicole had the power to fire Suzanne, she would've done it at that moment. Instead, she felt that Suzanne was undermining her authority and used this tragedy as her scapegoat to do it.

"What can I help with, Suzanne?" Beverly asked.

"Thank you for asking, but I will take care of it."

"Do you need anything from us?" Nicole asked.

Suzanne stood up, straightened out her uniform, and looked sharply at Nicole. "The only thing I need from you all is to have more compassion in these kinds of situations. The money will be there; be it at three hours or six, the money will always be there. Now, if there isn't anything else—" she paused for a response, and when she didn't get one, she walked out of the office with her head held high. Beverly revealed a subtle grin. She loved the way Suzanne handled them. It was perfect.

"Well, that was quite rude," Nicole said.

"How so?" Beverly turned towards Nicole.

"The way she responded. You didn't see anything wrong with that?" Nicole's eyebrows burrowed down.

"Actually, as her direct supervisor, no, I didn't. Put yourself in the shoes of that family. Their sister is in a coma, their mother just died, their father, forgive me for saying, is hopeless, and they have virtually no family here to support them through this process. Suzanne is probably the closest thing to a family they have right now. So yes, a little compassion goes a mighty long way. Rude is far from what that was. That what you just saw and heard, is pain."

Nicole didn't say shit else. She lowered her head and pretended to straighten out the papers on her lap as Beverly walked out of the office, leaving Nicole behind with Dr. Patel.

"Suzanne!" Beverly called out.

Suzanne turned back around and walked towards Beverly.

"Listen. I know what they said in there, but I'm telling you to give them more time. Has all of the family arrived?"

"Not to my knowledge."

"Either way. Leave them be until everyone they're expecting has had a

chance with her. If it comes back, I'll take the hit. Leave them be for now."
Beverly hugged Suzanne, and both of them went back to the nurse's station.

Raymelle and Raylina continued to sit quietly with their mother. Raylina sat at her bedside, and Raymelle sat in her rocking chair as his heart filled with sheer nothingness. He didn't know how or what to feel. He just knew his soul was emptied of everything except sorrow and pain, leaving him to feel powerless. He wanted so badly to blame someone for what he was feeling, but he knew God's hands were all up in it, and he wouldn't dare question that.

"Raymelle?" Raylina turned towards him. "What about daddy?"

"Man, I tried calling him mad times, and it keeps going to voicemail."

"So, what are we gonna do?"

"What chu mean?" He frowned.

"I mean, don't they have to come get momma? They can't keep her here forever. And what if they come and he still hasn't had a chance to see her?"

"Man, that's on him. I keep telling him about his phone. Nigga don't listen." Raymelle said as he stood to answer the knock at the door. "Charlyn." He gasped. He was so glad to see her. She wrapped her arms around him and tightly squeezed.

"How are you guys doing?" She walked over to Raylina and did the same.

"As good as we can be, I guess," Raymelle answered.

She looked over at Adala and was stunned at how beautiful she looked.

"She looks like a guardian angel, so beautiful and at peace. God bless and keep you, Mrs. Blevins." She softly said, turning back towards Raymelle. "Has anyone come to talk to you yet?"

"No. About what?" He asked.

"We have to get her transported to the funeral home soon and start getting things in motion. So, who do we talk to?" Charlyn inquired.

"Give me a minute." Raymelle walked out of the room and summonsed Suzanne to come down.

"Suzanne, this is Charlyn. She's Royelle's boss and attorney." Raymelle said when Suzanne entered the room.

"How are you, Suzanne? From past conversations with Royelle, I understand that all of Mrs. Blevins wishes for this moment have been documented in detail here. Therefore, we'd like to get that information so that we can make the appropriate arrangements."

"I would be more than happy to supply all of that to you, but Mr. Blevins has not arrived yet."

"We can't wait on him, Suzanne. I've been calling him since you called me, and his phone keeps going to voicemail." Raymelle said.

"I understand, and I'm sorry, Raymelle. But without him, we aren't able to do much. He's the Power of Attorney."

"No, he's not," Raymelle responded confusingly. "Royelle is. And obviously, she can't make any decisions right now." He continued.

"No, Raymelle. I'm afraid he is. Give me one second." Suzanne quickly walked back to the nurse's station, grabbed Royelle's file, and came right back.

"See. Your dad is Power of Attorney. He brought us these papers a week or so after Royelle went into the coma. I take it you all didn't know." Suzanne attempted to hand him all the court documents, but Charlyn grabbed the papers and began to thoroughly review them.

"She's right, Raymelle. Mr. Blevins has POA over everything related to her care and finances.

"This snake mutha—!" Raymelle caught himself remembering where he was and who he was standing in front of. And when he stormed out of the room, Suzanne and Charlyn followed.

"Raymelle. Let's go to the conference room." Suzanne suggested.

As they all walked over to the room, all the years of Rayford's bullshit and conniving ways came rushing to his mind side like ocean waters. At this point, he was done with his father. And if Rayford were standing before him, he would've felt the entire wrath of God from his son.

"Ok. Now explain this to me! Cause I'm confused."

"Raymelle, please. Take a deep breath. Suzanne isn't to blame here." Charlyn said.

"I'm not blaming her, Charlyn." He angrily responded as he paced back and forth, swallowing the fire seed of anger that had planted itself within him.

"Raymelle, I'm truly sorry. When he presented us with these documents, no one questioned it because he's her husband, and we knew Royelle was in the hospital. So, it made sense."

"She's right, Raymelle. With Royelle in the hospital, I'm sure it was effortless for him to show proof to the courts and contest her capability of making any decisions on your mothers' behalf."

"So, you're telling me that everything we do for my moms has to go through this snake ass coward?" He continued to pace the floors.

"That's what this says. It even gives your father full reign over everything connected to her." Charlyn answered.

"The fuck it does!" Raymelle snatched the papers out of Charlyn's hand. "Now, I don't know everything about her plans or money, but I know my moms didn't leave him in charge of shit, especially when it came to the funds. That snake can kiss my ass! So now what?!"

"Try calling your father again," Charlyn ordered.

Raymelle dialed out, and like before, it went straight to voicemail.

"Urghhhh!"

Raymelle forcibly threw his phone against the wall, and if it weren't for the Otterbox cover on it, it would've shattered into pieces from the impact. Charlyn feared what might happen next, and Suzanne was nervous about the whole situation.

"Look, this is what we can do. I called and left a voicemail, and you've tried calling several times, right?" Suzanne asked.

"Yea." Raymelle snapped back.

"Ok. We'll contact the funeral home and notify them that she's ready for transport. That will at least get her moved the right way and with dignity. If he puts up any fight, my voicemail will serve as a backup. But if this comes back…"

"It won't come back," Charlyn reassured. "And if it does, I have yours."

"Ok. Well, you all go back to the room, gather all of her belongings, and I will do my part. In the meantime, as far as anyone else is concerned, this conversation never happened, and Rayford authorized the move through his son. Understood?" Suzanne asked.

"Understood," Charlyn responded.

Everyone left the conference room with the understanding that Suzanne was going against the grain for Mrs. Blevins. It could cost her, her job, and all the years she put into that place, but she didn't care. She saw Rayford's deceit on the family, and it angered her.

An hour after Suzanne made the call, members from the John J. O'Connor funeral home in Dorchester had arrived to pick Adala up. When they saw the way she looked, it left them speechless. They had never seen anyone during transport as beautiful and mystified as Adala. The deceased was often in johnnies, nude, or regular clothing. This visual made them feel like they were already at the funeral.

Raylina sobbed profusely as the men carefully shifted Adala from her bed to their gurney. As a result, to help ease the pain that Raylina was experiencing, instead of using the standard black body bag, they covered Adala up from her neck to her feet with a thick White sheet, leaving her unblemished face uncovered.

"We just need a signature to approve the transport to the funeral home." One of the men passed the clipboard to Raymelle.

Raymelle was disgusted by the idea that he was even signing death release papers for his momma. Therefore, he quickly signed all the necessary spaces and handed the clipboard right back over. The man tore off Raymelle's copy and handed it to him.

"Here, Charlyn." He handed the papers over to her.

"Do you all have any questions before we leave?" One of the men asked.

Everyone shook their head no.

"You should be hearing from the funeral director in a few hours. At that time, she can answer any questions you might have and help to arrange her services. But if you need to reach her immediately, here's her business card." The man reached into the inside of his suit jacket, pulled out a business card, and handed it to Charlyn. "We'll be going now, and please accept our sincerest condolences. We'll take good care of her."

He shook Raymelle and Charlyn's hand and slowly transported Adala towards the backdoor, where all the deceased made their final exit. Suzanne, Mikino, and several other nurses stood at the door to say their final goodbyes. It made Raymelle feel so good inside. It reminded him that his mother was a great person, and even in her illness, she impacted people.

As soon as they opened the double doors, a massive ray of sunlight with Orange and Yellow hues overshadowed the exit. Suzanne smiled and quickly turned towards Raymelle, who was smiling right back at her. That was all the reassurance he needed to know that his mother was indeed an angel and at peace.

CHAPTER 11:
RAYFORD

The last walk down the hall and out of Angel Zone was heavy on Raymelle. The deep feeling of sadness felt paralyzingly numb. He cared about everything, but at the same time, cared about nothing. He wanted to be alone but hated the idea of feeling lonely. He hated everything about the way he was feeling at that moment. And the stares from all the nurses and staff didn't help at all. He wanted so badly to tell them to *fuck off,* but he understood the reasoning behind it.

"You doing ok, Raymelle?" Charlyn asked.

"Man Charlyn, I'm fucked up right now, but I'mma be a'ight. Just got a lot on my mind right now."

"I understand. So where are we headed to now?" She asked.

"I'm bout to go to my mother's house and see what's going on around there."

"I can tag along if you want. It might be helpful." She offered.

"Nah, it's cool. I'll call you if things get too crazy."

Before Charlyn could ask Raylina what she was doing, Raylina was already asking Charlyn if she could get a ride to Royelle's. She wasn't hip to everything going on, but she was smart enough to know that her father was up to some bullshit, and she didn't want any more parts of him or it. She vowed that she would do whatever was necessary to avoid him until Royelle was back home and on her feet.

Raymelle gave the green light to Charyln and handed her the keys to Royelle's place. He was happy Raylina didn't want to roll with him. He needed some alone time, and this was the perfect opportunity. He needed some time to think, some time to feel something, anything. He didn't want to admit it, but he felt utterly lost. If it wasn't for Charlyn, he wasn't quite sure where he'd be right now or what direction to go in.

Although he had his share of female friends, none of them was close enough to his family to call for help in a situation like this. His father was in no position to offer any type of advice or direction. He could barely keep up with something as small as a phone; giving him a responsibility such as planning a funeral was a recipe for disaster. Other than his sisters, he didn't fool with any of his family too much. And the boys he did have, he was sure, couldn't offer any help except with expenses.

When he got in his car, his cell phone automatically reconnected Pandora to the car's Bluetooth, and Boyz II Men's, One Sweet Day, played through the speakers. It was an instant reminder for him that his momma was ok. He was sure she was sending him a message through the cascade of sunlight she passed through on her way out in combination with the music.

It didn't sink in right away, but when it did, he screamed the loudest scream he could and punched on the steering wheel uncontrollably. Everything that had intensified inside of him came out with every yell and bang. It was the first time he had a moment to release all his emotions without conviction. What he was feeling, he wouldn't wish on his worst enemy. The motions of shock, pain, guilt, and anger made him feel like he was being cut into pieces. He didn't know why he was feeling that way, but a sense of himself was gone.

"Damn momma, man. Not only did you teach me how to live, now you're teaching me how to die. This shit hurts like hell man, for real." He continued to cry.

This was the most vulnerable Raymelle had ever been in any situation. He felt unhinged when he learned about Royelle, but this, this was different.

This was an unexplainable level of pain. The kind of pain that words could never match. The only way to understand it was if you went through it yourself, and sometimes that didn't even matter.

After several minutes he finally pulled himself together, put the car in drive, and began the ride back to Dorchester in a zoned-out state of mind. It was a pure case of highway hypnosis. He knew there were cars around him, knew they were in motion, but he couldn't see them. He was driving with no sense of direction but yet knew where he was going. He tried to think about everything that he needed to do for his mother, but his mind kept recircling back to the sight of her being wheeled out the back door of Angel Zone under a radiance of sunshine.

"It's your beauty, momma. It's always been your beauty." He slightly smiled.

As he got closer to the Loma, his nerves began to increase, perspiration met his underarms, and thousands of tiny sweat beads began formulating on his forehead. He didn't know if he should be mad or be grateful that Rayford finally stepped up to do something. While he tried to fight off the increasing urge to spazz on his father, he also tried to understand the reasoning behind his father's antics. Despite this, his only goal now was to follow through with his mother's last wishes. The Power of Attorney scheme meant nothing.

When he drove onto the street, it was quiet as usual. But, with only three houses on the block, that was expected. There were no neighbors in sight, and the only car on the street was Rayford's beat-up Toyota Camry. Raymelle got out of the truck, shaking his head. He was incensed when he saw all the trash in front of the house and in the yard. If he didn't know any better, he would've thought the house was unoccupied. Knowing how Adala kept the home inside and out, compared to what it looked like now, pissed him off. But that was a discussion for another time.

He used his keys to let himself him in and instantly grew disgusted. The house reeked of spoiled food and stale cigarettes, the dishes were piled up in and around the sink, and for the first time in the house, he saw roaches crawling everywhere in the kitchen.

"Unfucking-believable." He said, making his way to the living room.

He was sickened to see all the clothes thrown all over the couches. There was so much of it that it was impossible to tell the clean from the dirty clothes apart. The ashtrays were full of everything from cigarette buds to candy wrappers and water. *'This shit is a fucking mess!'* He thought as he continued to scan the area of all its messes.

He grabbed the opened and unopened mail that was sprawled all over the coffee table and started reading through some of it. "The fuck?" He whispered when he read all the termination notices for the utilities due to lack of payment, and the foreclosure letters on the house didn't make things any better. He sighed and folded up the most recent ones, sticking them in his pocket. As he continued going through the mail, he noticed that anything addressed to Adala was unopened, except for the Fidelity Life insurance letters. Suddenly his eyes blazed with fire as he began to read each letter:

"Thank you for your recent inquiry on increasing your policy. To better serve you and your needs, we ask that you please visit one of our local offices with your unexpired identification card."

Raymelle was vexed. He couldn't imagine who would've requested such a thing, but all roads led to Rayford. He grabbed all the letters from Fidelity, stuck them in his pocket, and went to his parent's bedroom.

"Pops!" He yelled, covering his nose as he swung open the door.

Rayford didn't budge.

"Pops!" He said louder.

"Mmm." Rayford groaned.

"Man, wake up!"

"Wah de hell yuh wa?!" Rayford mumbled.

"Wake up! We gotta talk!"

"Suh early inna de mawnin?! Wah de hell ah wrang wid yuh?!"

Raymelle, having no compassion or sympathy left for Rayford, blurted out, "Man, ain't shit wrong me! Other than the fact that Ma died this morning!"

"Huh? Wat yuh seh!" Rayford sat up in the bed.

"Now, do I have your attention?!"

"Nuh fuck wid me bwoy!"

"Do I look like I'm fucking with you?!" Raymelle snapped back.

Rayford stopped mumbling under his breath long enough to look at his son's face and when he saw the look of anguish, he knew it was real.

"Oh mi God! Please nuh tell mi dat! Wah mek nobody call mi?!"

"I've been calling you all morning! A.Z. been calling you all morning! Where the hell is your phone?!" Raymelle yelled back.

"Ova dere!" Rayford pointed to the dresser that sat across from the foot of the bed against the wall.

"It ain't helping shit if it's over here, is it?" Raymelle grabbed the phone and sucked his teeth when he realized it was off. "A lot of good this does, huh?" He pressed the power button on the side, and once it came on, the flashing blue light for voicemail notifications came on. "Man. See this shit. Check ya damn voicemails, man." Raymelle threw the phone on the bed.

"Bwoy, Mi nuh ave time fi yuh shit!" Rayford replied in a stern voice.

Raymelle gagged as his father rose out of bed. The pungent smell of shit hit his nostrils like a ton of bricks. To see his father looking and smelling like he did disgusted Raymelle. It was clear that whatever Rayford was going through had a hold of him, and it made Raymelle very uncomfortable.

"Son pass mi dem pants." Rayford pointed to the khaki pants thrown on the floor in front of the dresser.

"For what? You need to get in the shower Pops for real. You look and smell like you ain't showered in days." Raymelle turned his nose up.

"Mind yuh biznizz bwoy an pass mi dem damn pants. Yuh nuh kno wah yuh a talk about!"

"Yea a'ight. I know what I see and smell, though, and this house is a mess. It stinks, and honestly, no one should be living here. What you been doing, Pops? Raymelle questioned.

"Bwoy! I already said, mind your business! Now! Mi nuh ave time fi ah shower! Mi need tuh git tuh Angel Zone!"

"Pops, listen. There's no need to go to Angel Zone. It's already been taken care of. The people came and picked her up already. We need to get down to the funeral home."

Rayford stopped what he was doing, his eyes furrowed, and he shot a quizzical look at Raymelle."Wah duh yuh mean? I have to sign the papers fi har tuh bi released. Mi neva give anyone permission tuh duh dat!"

Rayford flip-flopped between dialects constantly. And somehow felt like he was more in demand and control when he did. He figured if he couldn't get across what he was saying in Patois, it would be better understood and more forceful in English. Neither worked. As kids, Raymelle and his sisters took it seriously. Now, as adults, they found him to be a joke. His bantering was old and no longer a threat.

"Your permission? She had to be moved by a certain time, and since you didn't answer or respond, I gave them the permission to move her."

"Yuh?! Ow dem allow yuh tuh make that decision?"

"What you meannn how? I'm her son! That's how."

" An mi har Powa of Attorney!" Rayford shot back.

It was at that moment, he realized he had just put his foot in his mouth, but it was too late. Raymelle was all over it; it was the window of opportunity he needed.

"Since when?" Royelle's POA. When did that change?"

Raymelle pretended not to know the truth. He wanted to see how far he could go with his father, hoping his father would be straight up and honest with him.

"Dat nuh matta. It need fi be dun." Rayford waved off. "Jus tek mi tuh di funeral yaad."

"What do you mean it doesn't matter? It does matter. Seems li—

"Boy! Shut up! I mean it, Raymelle! Shut the hell up! Did it matter to you when your sister did it to me?! Did it?! Just shut up!" Rayford shouted in his heavy accent.

Raymelle burned his eyes into Rayford, and Rayford purposely avoided eye contact as he headed towards the shower. He could feel the heat on his neck. He knew he had fucked up, and Raymelle was on to him. The last thing he ever wanted to do was lose his only son's confidence, but little did he know he was already about two hours too late. The more Raymelle began to see his father's true colors, the more Raymelle's dislike towards him grew.

Raymelle walked into his old room to find it exactly how he left it, clean as a whistle. Nothing had been moved or misplaced. It felt good to have that space to unwind in. He couldn't do it anywhere else in the house, so it was well-suited. He laid back on his old bed, and all the memories he had with his mother in that house came rushing back. He tried to put them on pause, but it was impossible. Her loving and dotting ways continued to resurface.

He tried to remember the times when she was mean, hit him, or yelled, and there were none. All he could remember was the good in her. The redirection or punishment she had ever given her kids was always full of reasoning, and that was the one thing that made them love her more. Her love and understanding for her kids were untouchable; Rayford could never compare. She believed in the taking away and earning back system; Rayford believed in ass-whoopings and tough love. They weren't the same.

"Yuh ready bwoy?" Rayford asked, looking like the only thing that touched the water was his feet.

"Are you sure you're ready? That was a real fast shower."

"I've had about enough of your shit and your smart ass mouth." Rayford shot back.

Raymelle got up, looked him up and down, and walked past him like he wasn't shit. The whole ride to O'Connor's, Rayford called everyone under the sun to inform of Adala's passing. His phone was so loud that Raymelle could hear everything the person on the other end was saying. Some people were genuinely sympathetic, while others were more concerned about the house, inquiring about funeral expenses and how the family was going to pay for everything.

It annoyed Raymelle to hear his father on the phone with all the people he knew his mother didn't mess with. And although he had the urge to snatch the phone from his father and cuss everyone out, he stayed quiet to keep things peaceful and continued to focus on the road, pretending not to hear what was going on.

Finally, they arrived at the funeral home, and Raymelle took a deep breath. He parked the truck, turned off the engine, and unbuckled his seatbelt. When he noticed Rayford wasn't budging, he asked, "are you coming?" Rayford cut his eyes over at Raymelle and turned his attention back to the front entrance of the funeral home.

For the first time, Raymelle could see Rayford's sorrow; whether it was real or not remained to be seen. Raymelle got out of the truck, closed the door, and leaned on the front grill waiting on his father. After five good minutes, Rayford got out and started walking to the front door without a word to Raymelle. Raymelle just shook his head and started walking behind him.

"Hello, Sir. How can I help you?" The Administrative Assistant asked.

"I'm here about Adala Blevins," Rayford responded.

"Yes, sir. Let me get the Funeral Director, Joann, for you. Please have a seat. She'll be right with you."

Since Rayford thought he had it all under control, Raymelle stood back and let him lead. He sat down on one of the lobby chairs, thrilled at his mother's decision to pick this funeral home. He was impressed by the artwork on the wall, the wallpaper design, and the overall maintenance of the place. He was so used to being at the hood funeral homes that he thought all funeral homes looked the same, with that fucked up pale blue or ugly flower wallpaper design. It was already a sad situation to lay a loved one to rest, but going into a funeral home that had a somber look and feel made it worse.

"Good Morning, gentlemen." Joann greeted.

"Good Morning," Raymelle replied. Rayford didn't say a word.

"Please follow me to my office."

Raymelle hated being there. The funeral home itself gave him the creeps. Not to mention, dead bodies surrounded it, his mother being one of them.

"Please. Have a seat." Joann waited for them to get settled before she sat. "First, allow me to express my deepest condolences to you both and to your family."

"Thank you," Raymelle replied. Again Rayford didn't say a word.

"I understand that you all are here on behalf of Mrs. Blevins, correct?"

"Yes," Raymelle answered.

"And if I may, can I please have your names and your relationship to the deceased?"

"I'm her son Raymelle, and that's my father, her husband, Rayford."

"Very nice to meet you both. I hate that it's under these circumstances, but glad to meet you nonetheless. I am more than happy to get those affairs in order. Let's start with the —"

"Cost." Rayford rudely interrupted. "She had life insurance. So, I need to know how much this is gonna cost.

Raymelle gave his father a knife-piercing look. Rayford was so dry and direct that it gave off the feel of someone who didn't care and just wanted whatever needed to happen to be done with already. Aside from that, he kept using the word "I" as if he was the one who was going to forego all of the expenses.

"You'd be pleased to know that she left no expense or debt." Joann gladly opened Adala's file.

"Excuse me," Rayford said. "Waah shi chat bout son?" Rayford looked at Raymelle with a surprised look. Raymelle stayed silent, waiting to hear what Joann would say next.

"Yes, sir. She came in and paid for her services during the early stages of her diagnosis. Later, she came back with a notarized letter signed by her and her attorneys detailing how she wanted her services."

"Attorneys! Let me see that!" Rayford snatched the folder from in front of Joann.

"Chill out, Pops."

"Bwoy nuh tell mi wah fi duh!"

Rayford turned his attention back to the papers, and just as Joann had stated, Adala had everything she wanted to be done itemized in Black and White. Her final wishes were straight and to the point. There was no room for error. And everything, as Joann said, was paid in full.

"I don't understand." He puzzlingly looked at Joann.

"What it states is—."

"Ma'am! Ma'am! I know what it says." Rayford rudely horned in.

Joann remained quiet and stayed professional.

"Pops, let me see that."

Raymelle couldn't believe what he was reading, but his heart smiled the more he read. He loved how his mother made sure that there was no stone unturned when it came to her. And more so, it put Rayford in charge of nothing. Again!

"So, my mother only wants ten people at her service and cremation?"

"Yes, sir. She limited the service to ten people of your choosing, not including the five of you. Totaling 15 people max."

"That's bullshit!" Rayford blurted out.

"Pops!"

Raymelle was annoyed and embarrassed by his father's barbarity. He couldn't understand what the problem was, and he really didn't give a fuck. He was sick of his father's behaviors and disrespect towards Joann. Being struck with grief was not an excuse or pardon to become an asshole. His behavior was childish and uncalled for.

"So what about all of my friends? They won't be able to come?" Rayford asked.

"Pops, that's just it. Those are YOUR friends. None of those people were ma's friends. That lady knew what she was doing, and we're gonna respect that."

"Boyyy! I'm telling you! Don't say shit else!" Rayford spat.

Joann looked on as the two of them went back and forth. She was unmoved by Rayford and respected Raymelle for trying to defuse the situation.

"Ms. Joann, as you were saying." Raymelle ignored his father's false threats. " My mother. You said she paid for everything? Service, casket, cremation, everything?" Raymelle asked, wanting to be sure he completely understood.

"Yes. That is correct."

Raymelle cracked a smile.

"What's so funny?" Rayford asked irritability

"The fact that moms was always on her shit. Excuse my language, Joann."

Rayford sucked his teeth as only a Jamaican knew how.

"So, we don't owe you any money?" Rayford asked.

"No, sir. It's all paid. All I need from you is the date, time, a few signatures, and we're good to go. Once she's cremated, the urn will be ready for pick up, or we can ship it out. Whichever is easiest."

While he was putting on a show for them, Rayford was ecstatic that Adala paid for and organized everything on the low, which meant more money for him once the insurance paid out. It was a win-win situation, or so he thought.

"What's the soonest?" Rayford asked.

"Since there is no autopsy to be had, we could do this Friday or Saturday afternoon."

"Friday," Rayford quickly answered.

"Sounds good. If you, Mr. Blevins, could sign these forms for me, I would greatly appreciate it."

Raymelle stayed quiet and watched as his father signed form after form without asking what he was signing. But, he figured, if his mother went this far to get things legitly done, then the paperwork he was signing had to be just as legit.

"We're all set. Do either of you have any other questions for me?" Joann asked.

"When can I see my wife?"

"Once she is ready, I can arrange a time for you to come back. Who should I call when she's ready?"

"Me. I'm Power of Attorney," Rayford said with authority.

He reached over Joann's desk, grabbed her notepad and pen, and wrote his number down. Joann noticing his overtone took the paper and acknowledged his statement. As soon as he got the confirmation he needed, he walked out without saying thank you or shaking her hand. She wasn't offended, though. She had been in the business long enough to know when someone was overplaying their part, spouses included.

The idea that Rayford felt like he had some type of power irritated the hell out of Raymelle. Had Rayford been looking at the bigger picture, he would've realized, as everyone else did in the office, that even in her hour of death, his wife was in total control and commanded it from her spirit.

"Sorry about all that," Raymelle said when Rayford left.

"Oh, don't be. When your mother was first diagnosed, she and I became very good friends, and she told me a lot about your father. Trust me; I was expecting that reaction from him." She smiled. "Are you gonna be ok, though?"

"Yea, I'm good.

"Well, if there is anything else you need, you have both of my numbers, do not hesitate to call me." They hugged, and Raymelle walked out.

CHAPTER 12:
RESURFACE

A few days had passed since Raymelle had spoken to or seen
Rayford. His focus was to ensure that Adala's service was
carried out the way she wanted it and done respectfully. But,
when his phone began blowing up at 6:45 the morning of his mother's service, he
knew it was something. When he reached over to grab it, he was surprised to see
it was his father. Knowing it was uncommon and sporadic for Rayford to be
calling him at that particular hour, he knew bullshit was on the horizon.

"What's up, Pop." He faintly answered.

"Mi tell dat uhman tuh call mi dis mawnin!" He hollered.

Raymelle wiped the cold out of his eyes while his father continued
yelling. He personally didn't give two fucks about any of it. It was too early
in the morning for one, for two, his ramblings made absolutely no sense,
and for three, he was already on Raymelle's shit list. Yelling into his ear
about trivial shit was only making matters worse.

Raymelle put the phone down on the other pillow and let his father go on
and on about him needing to spend time with Adala by himself. In Raymelle's
opinion, Rayford was either looking for a reason to be bitter, a reason to fight,
or this was his dense mechanism of dealing with Adala's passing. And although

Raymelle understood his father's position, it didn't call for everything he was doing.

"Raymelle! Yuh hear mi a talk tuh yuh bwoy!?"

"I hear you, Pops, but you ain't talking; you're yelling, and it's not even seven in the morning."

"Mi nuh kya! Call that uhman an tell har I'll be there in an hour!"

"Fuck!"

Raymelle slammed the phone down on the bed, infuriated. Not only was he rudely awakened out of his sleep, but it was also the day of his mother's service, and all he wanted to do was get through the day. He dialed out to Joann.

"Good Morning, this is Joann." She gracefully answered.

He breathed a sigh of relief. "Good Morning Joann, this is Raymelle."

"Hi, Raymelle. How can I help you?"

"I wanted to let you know my pops will be there in an hour, and he's upset."

Joann's eyebrows frowned. "Oh? May I ask about what?"

"He said something about never getting a call." Raymelle made sure to choose his words and tone wisely. He didn't want to sound upset or accusatory.

"Actually, Raymelle, your dad had a three-hour one-on-one visit with your mother the day after we met. He asked if he could do another one-on-one for today, and we agreed. I called your dad several times last night to set up a meeting, and each time he answered, he hung up on us before we could say anything. If I may say something, and I hope I don't offend you." She politely said.

"Go 'head." He responded.

"His words slurred each time he did speak, and he seemed a bit incoherent."

Soon as those words rolled off her lips, Rayford's irrationality started to make sense. '*I should've known better,*' Raymelle thought. He felt stupid and humiliated for even mentioning it to her. He apologized to Joann and advised her to keep him posted if his father got up there tripping with them. She let Raymelle know they had everything under control, and Rayford could come at any time.

Raymelle grunted in agitation as he hung up the phone. He felt like he always had to be on guard when it came to his father. Since the day Adala was sent to Angel Zone, Rayford's intoxication heavily increased, making him more temperamental, random, and at times unstable. His attitude was so unpredictable that the idea of having to babysit him or apologize to others for his behavior was sickening.

When he called Rayford back, he answered the phone with an attitude as if the problem was Raymelle's. One thing he never liked to do was take accountability for anything he did. And if it looked like a finger might be pointed at him for any reason, he found a way to reverse it right back to the person who was pointing at him. But Raymelle wasn't the one. He told his father to take his ass to the funeral home and not to cause those people any problems. But Rayford didn't listen. Instead, he talked over his son as if everything he said had no meaning.

Since his sleep was already disrupted, Raymelle decided to get up and get his day started. He walked over to Royelle's room, and from the smell of it, he could tell that Raylina had already showered and was more than likely dressed. When he called out her name, she came out of the kitchen and presented herself at the bottom of the staircase fully dressed with hair done just as he suspected.

"What you doing?" He asked.

"Making something to eat. You want something?"

"Nah, I'm good. I'm about to go handle my business, and then we out."

"Ok." She responded.

Raylina was confused about why they would be leaving so early, but she didn't bother to question him about it. She had no more fight in her. She already woke up restless with her mind stuck on Royelle and her mother. She exhausted herself with her thoughts, trying to piece together why God would allow her family to go through so much at the same time. She hated the idea that Royelle couldn't be a part of their mother's final good-byes; it felt so wrong. It felt like it was out of its natural order of how things were supposed to be. Her mother dying while Royelle was in a coma just wasn't right.

Raylina finished cooking her breakfast, went into the family room, and turned the television to CNN. It was always the same bullshit with them and every other news channel; sadness. She wondered how they could endure so much of the information they take in and not be sad or angry about it. The world was fucked up in her eyes, and the only thing that brought any sanity to it was her family and rain.

With her family, good or bad, they were perfect to her. She found goodness in all of them, despite any drama or shortcomings. Being with and around them made her feel alive, loved, and unblemished of flaws from the world around her. There was nothing that they could do that would make her love them any less, and they made her feel the same way, no matter how many times in life she fucked up.

The rain stood second best to her family. Like her older sister, she absolutely loved it. Any time it rained, her soul danced. It cleansed her mind and spirit whenever she saw its millions of droplets fall from the limitless sky, smelled the air, or heard the beating of its beads on the windowsill or ground. Adala always told her girls that when it rained, it was God's way of refreshing the earth, making way for something new. And the sisters both lived by that.

After two hours off waiting, the two headed out, and a short period later, they were at their parent's home. When they arrived, Raylina was baffled. She didn't understand the reason for being there when they should've been on their way to the funeral home. But, she was done trying to figure out everyone else's madness when she had her own to deal with. When they got inside, Raymelle couldn't believe what he was seeing. He didn't know how Rayford pulled it off, but the house was immaculately clean. There wasn't shit Raymelle could say or complain about.

"Damnnn!" Raylina said, shocked to see the house the way it was. "Who the hell did this? Cause I know, he didn't." She continued.

"Facts, sis," Raymelle replied, continuing to walk through the house.

He checked each room, and they were all spotless, to his surprise. Each had been swept, mopped, adorned with new clean linens, and blessed with the Clean Linen scent Glade plug-ins, giving the house a fresh and clean aroma. It didn't look or smell like it had a few days prior, leaving Raymelle speechless. It was as if Rayford had a eureka moment.

"So, is he planning a party or something that we don't know about?" Raylina questioned.

"I don't know, sis. I'm just glad the house is clean. It looks like momma's way of cleaning, right?"

This was the first time in a long time, that Rayford put any care and thought into the place. As they looked around, the way the house looked and smelled brought them great joy and sadness when they remembered everything their mother was and how she raised and loved them.

Joy for all the years she was nothing less than perfect to them, and sadness knowing that they had lost their mother the day she could no longer remember their names. It didn't matter that she had an absent mind; her presence alone was all they needed to know everything was all right in their world. Her being gone permanently was the icing on the cake to their sorrow.

They stayed a bit longer, looking through all the picture albums while noticing a reoccurrence of Rayford's absence in most of the photos. And when he was in the picture, the despondency between him and Adala was abundantly clear. It was apparent that both of them were extremely unhappy with the other. Neither of their smiles was as bright as one would expect from the parents' in a family photo. But like a lot of families that they knew, the parents' stayed together because of complacency, or for the sake of the kids, not because of love.

And if one paid attention to Adala's beautiful Green eyes, sadness surrounded them when Rayford was present. Only when she was pictured with her children did the gleam of Emerald present itself. Her gentleness, honesty, innocence, and purity were so vibrant and free when Rayford wasn't in the picture. Her being freed of him, was harmony in its prime.

Before leaving the house, Raymelle gathered the albums that contained most of the pictures with Adala in them, and Raylina took the 8x10 photo of the four of them dressed in all white; it was her and Royelle's favorite. No Rayford. Just Adala and her kids.

The ride to O'Connor's was quiet. They didn't know what the other was thinking, but they equally related to the dead air. They understood it for each other. It was like a sibling thing. Although years apart, their connection to the same mother, being carried in the same womb, with the same amount of love, had a connection all of its own. Like they didn't know what the other was thinking, but they knew. The silence to them was as if speaking words out loud. When Raymelle looked over at Raylina, she saw him out of her peripheral and looked back at him.

"We got this, sis. I know how you feel. And we got this. Royelle's gon' be ok. We gon' be ok." Raymelle reassured his sister.

She cracked a small smile and looked back out the passenger side window. She knew he was right. But at the moment, she wasn't ok. She wanted to be. But she wasn't.

"Brother, who are all these people?" She asked when they arrived at the funeral home and found the parking lot full of cars and many others double-parked on the street.

"I don't know, sis." He circled the block a few times and finally found parking.

It wasn't common for a funeral home to have two funerals going on simultaneously, but O'Connor's was different. The funeral home was so big that they could tailor a traditional funeral service and a memorial service followed by cremation at the same time. Since Adala wanted something simple and small, O'Connor's was more than happy to appease her and meet the needs of her family.

While the customary funeral was taking place in the main front room, Adala's service was being held in the back room, which was big enough to fit the casket and twenty chairs max. There was no standing room allowed. Services like Adala's were very easy to manage, as far as foot traffic was concerned. They required less assistance and manpower in comparison to the traditionary services.

From a distance, Raymelle and Raylina could see lots of people outside, some consoling one another, others were smoking, some were on their phones or simply standing alone, reflecting. But when they got inside the funeral home, the crowd was far worse. It was packed with people from corner to corner, making it difficult to walk through without bumping someone or stepping on their heels.

As Raymelle walked towards the back room where his mother was, he took a quick glimpse into the main room, and his heart sunk when he saw two caskets, one belonging to a child. He knew his pain could not compare to what that family and their friends were experiencing. The loss of an adult was one thing, but the loss of a child, at any age, was something completely different. When Raymelle finally made it to the building's backside, Joann was standing near the door while her other staff manned the main room.

"How are you, Raymelle?" She gently greeted.

"I'm good, Joann."

"You must be Raylina." Joann smiled.

Raylina silently nodded.

Did he make it?" Raymelle asked.

"Yes. He's in there. He came in quietly and has been sitting with her ever since. But, I'll be out here if you need anything." She opened the door and closed it behind them when they walked in.

Rayford was sitting in the first row directly in front of Adala, while Charlyn, Jacob, Suzanne, and a few of Rayford's friends occupied the other seats. From the looks of it, it appeared Rayford didn't put any forethought into the limit of fifteen. As usual, it was always about him. When Rayford turned towards Raylina and Raymelle, they could tell that Rayford had been crying something awful. His eyes were bloodshot red and swollen, a dead giveaway that his tough-guy persona was being called into question.

"What's up, Pops? You a'ight?" Raymelle whispered, gently patting his father on the back.

"Yah. Mi criss."

Raylina walked directly to the casket without saying a word to her father. She was annoyed by him and all the accommodations that had to be made to pacify his behaviors. If it was exhausting for her, she could imagine how Raymelle must've felt. While they waited for the priest to arrive, they both went around hugging and thanking people for coming before taking their seats.

Once they sat down, they were so quiet in their thoughts; you could hear a pin drop. Even Rayford, who was a complete ass towards Adala most times, was deeply pained by her passing more than he cared to admit. He knew he wouldn't be where he was if it wasn't for her. The support, encouragement, and love that she gave him, despite him not reciprocating it, was gone for good, and that was distressing for him.

"Ma'am! Ma'am! This is a private viewing. The service you're looking for is upfront."

Everyone turned when they heard Joann's elevated voice. Raylina took a huge gasp.

"Xandraaaa!" She yelled.

She rushed towards Xandra, causing her to stumble back a few steps from the force Raylina applied when she hugged her. Xandra slowly looked over at Joann with a screwed-up *bitch please* expression and turned her attention back to Raylina. Joann looked over at Raymelle, who nodded his head in approval. She apologized to Xandra and to the family for the disturbance and walked out.

Raylina continued to hold Xandra tightly. She didn't want to let go. Xandra was the closest thing to a sister she had, and she needed her now more than ever. Charlyn cracked a smile when she saw her. This was exactly what Raylina needed, she thought. Xandra showing up couldn't have come at a much better time. Raymelle on the other hand wasn't moved by her presence.

"Where have you been?" Raylina cried. "Royelle is in a coma. We don't know for how long. She was in an accident and—"

"Shhh. I know, baby. I know." Xandra consoled.

Raylina rambled on so fast that she could barely breathe. She was so excited to see Xandra that she began repeating the things she had already told her through messenger. Xandra kissed Raylina on the forehead, and before sitting down, walked to the casket and kneeled before Adala. It gave her chills seeing Adala look so beautiful and at peace. But, it hurt her like hell to be viewing the body of the one woman who taught her how to be one. She said a short prayer, stood up and walked towards Raymelle, who was standing a few feet away from Rayford. Rayford's anger quickly ignited as she got closer. Everything that was calm in him went out the window at the sight of her.

"What are you doing here?! You think you can just come and go when you want?!" Rayford snapped.

To avoid any further confusion or embarrassment for Rayford, Xandra looked at him through her dark shades with discourse and fire in her eyes, said nothing, and took a seat in the back of the room, furthest away from him.

"Girl! I said, what are you doing here!?"

"Pops, chill out, man." Raymelle tried to calm him. "We're all here for ma."

"Dis ah mi wife! Wollah yuh can cut!"

"Pops, ain't nobody leaving. She's our mother too."

To avoid whooping Rayford's ass where he stood, Xandra got up and gathered her things. "Bro. I'll be outside. Bye momma. I love you." She kissed the fingertips on her right hand and gently blew the kiss in Adala's direction before walking out.

"Pops, Why you do that man? She ain't do nothing to you. You're wrong, yo."

Raymelle walked out to find Xandra while Rayford continued on his rant. He was so embarrassed. Of all the times for Rayford to act a plum fool, he chose this unfortunate time. One by one, the guest who weren't connected to Rayford got up, paid their final respects, and left out. Those cool with Rayford sat back and enjoyed the show waiting to see what would happen next. Acting a complete ass was the type of shit he was known for doing around them, and they were all for it, even if it was during a funeral. It was just something more to gossip about when they got around all their other drunk friends. Once Raymelle got past the main room's crowd, he quickly spotted Xandra posted up in front of a mailbox across the street from the funeral home. From a distance, she could see he was heated. *'Oh boy,'* she thought, knowing he was about to come for neck.

"What the fuck, yo! Where the fuck you been?!" He threw his hands up in a rage.

"Come on with it bro, Get it all out now cause this is the only chance you're gonna get," Xandra said.

"What the fuck is that supposed to mean?"

"I'm just saying. Say what you need to say now cause we're not revisiting this shit."

"Xandra, on some real nigga shit, I don't know who the fuck you think you're talking to, and maybe wherever the fuck you disappeared to helped you grow some balls, but you better watch how you handle me."

"Ok." Xandra sarcastically replied rolling her eyes.

Raymelle was never the kind to put his hands on women, but he was itching to bash her face in. She thought she was untouchable, and Raymelle wanted so badly to show her otherwise. On the other hand, Xandra respected Raymelle a great deal, but she didn't take kindly to idle threats, no matter who they came from. She was letting him make it, on the strength of everything that was going on, but there was only so much she was willing to tolerate.

"Do you even know what the fucks been going on?!"

"As a matter of fact brother, I do know. And to answer your question, I was on vacation."

"Vacation? Really Xandra? You really want me to believe that bullshit? A'ight."

"Raymelle does any of that really matter right now. What matters is y'all two and Royelle. Period."

"How did you even know we were here?"

"Nigga, social media. How the fuck else!? Raylina been inboxing me damn near every day since I've been gone. I just saw the messages late last night when I got back." She lied.

Raymelle didn't believe a word of her story, but he couldn't argue facts that he didn't have. So he continued to let her talk until Raylina joined them. She let Raymelle know that she was ready to go because her father was inside of the funeral home tripping, and she wanted no parts of it. Raymelle huffed at his father's annoyance and told Xandra to take Raylina back to Royelle's place, and he would meet them there. Xandra obliged.

The girls walked towards Xandra's Audi truck, and Raymelle walked back inside. When he got to the room, Rayford's drunken friends were conversing amongst themselves as if at a fun event, while Rayford was sitting in the same spot as before, having a full-blown conversation with Adala as if she could respond. Raymelle was beside himself.

He walked over to the casket, and Rayford moved over, allowing Raymelle a moment. He kissed his mother several times on the forehead, cheek, and hand and asked her to forgive him for not staying longer. But, there was no way they would continue tolerating their father's disrespect. He kissed her a few more times, pulled his phone out, and took some pictures to show Royelle whenever she was ready.

"Aye. You only got a few hours left with her. Enjoy them while you can, and don't cause these people any more problems. And y'all," he pointed at Rayford's friends. "Keep the noise down for real. You're at a funeral, not a party." Everyone, including Rayford, gave Raymelle a scornful look as he walked out to find Joann.

"Hey, Joann. He tapped her on the shoulder.

"Hey. Everything ok?" She softly asked.

"Not really. Me and my sister are leaving. I don't know how much longer he plan's on staying. But if he gives y'all any problems, call the police."

"Raymelle? What happened?" Joann was stunned by what he said.

"Joann, thank you for everything, but we're out. If you need anything else from me, you got my number. But if it involves him, call the police, don't call me." Raymelle gave her a hug and dipped.

CHAPTER 13:
IT'S ALL CONNECTED

A tall and handsome, African-American Detective Jayson Aveen was thirty-five years young, with eight years on the force, three in homicide. Yet, he was still very vibrant, active, muscular, always up for a challenge, eager to learn, and desperate to solve his very first murder. But he knew what he was up against working for the Milton Police Department, so he was always one step ahead of the game, working much harder than those around him. This was his make-it-or-break-it case, and he was not only determined to solve it but also eager to remove Royelle's name from the possible list of suspects connected to it.

When he first joined homicide, he remembered being told that he would come across that one case that he would never be able to forget; he genuinely believed Trevion's case was that case. As he sat at his kitchen table preparing to review crime scene photos, the sounds of Royelle's agonizing screams, the tears, and the level of disbelief that was written all over her face flashed in his mind. And even though police officers were trained to take emotion out of the equation, he couldn't help but feel somewhat responsible for Royelle's mental and emotional break.

As he analyzed the crime scene photos, he shook his head while looking back at Trevion and Bella's interactions. "This shit is a mess," he said, still in disbelief that Bella could be connected, but the proof was in the pudding. Anyone who was around a murder victim right before they died was automatically affiliated whether they wanted to be or not.

He sat and wondered how he got himself caught up in such a situation. The last thing he wanted was to be tied to a murder suspect who was, for lack of better words, a hoe. And no matter how much he missed her and craved for her, staying as far away from Bella as possible was the best thing for him. It didn't matter how much he loved her vibe and sex; he loved his career more. And losing everything because of their dealings with one another was not an option.

He continued to study the pictures as if they would come alive for him if he just starred a little longer. He was convinced that something was going to stand out. It had too. There were just too many things in the photos for nothing to offer a clue. There had to be something everyone was overlooking, and he was intent on finding out what that something was.

He read all the reports and statements, and everything seemed like horse-shit. No one knew anything. It was the typical, see something, say nothing, hood motto. Angrily, he screamed and threw everything off the table. He was so indignant at the idea of knowing the answers were right in front of him, but yet, he couldn't pinpoint it.

Here was his first opportunity to solve a murder, and he couldn't piece anything together. All he needed was one lead to point him in the right direction, but nothing was hitting. So to calm his nerves and try to relax, he grabbed his Burbon, his snifter Whiskey glass, and filled it damn near to the rim. Normally, the glass would be less than half full, but less than half full wasn't going to cut it in this situation.

As he sipped slowly, two thoughts plagued him. First, he knew Royelle wasn't involved but felt like she had to know something. According to all the people they interviewed, Royelle was his right-hand woman. So, in theory, the way Jayson saw it, she had to know his enemy's, financial problems, something, anything that would explain why someone would want him dead. People didn't just go around killing other people for nothing. There was always a motive behind it.

Secondly, his other wife, Aruba, identifying him further puzzled Jayson. He couldn't wrap his mind around the fact that neither woman knew about the other. So that, too, had to be a lie. But giving Royelle's reaction, cop's intuition let him know; she really didn't know. But, how could this man live a double life in the same state and not get caught up, he wondered? Boston was way too small, and people talked way too often. But then again, some men just had all the charm and smarts to pull off certain shit. It was clear to Jayson that Trevion was one of those guys.

It made him wonder what it was that each woman brought to the table. Men who led double lives did so with a benefit in mind. They didn't just do it for fun. If that were the case, then the men who carried on double-lives would just join the women together and build a Poly relationship of sorts. That wasn't this. Jayson was sure Trevion had an ulterior motive. Unfortunately, he wasn't alive to tell the story. But he knew that one of the women, if not both, had some kind of information. It was all connected somehow; he just had to dig a little bit deeper.

He sipped a little more and finally calmed down enough to let his brain unravel itself and collect its thoughts; that's when the idea of reaching back out to Aruba came to mind. Since Royelle couldn't answer any questions, then surely Aruba could. Besides, she was the one listed as his next of kin, the one who provided his dental records, and the one who stood to gain the most since she was technically his real wife, at least on paper at the hospital.

Although she provided a solid Alibi of her being in Chicago at the time of the murder, it didn't exclude her from being a suspect. She was always a suspect. The spouses usually are. Hell, everybody connected to the victim was a suspect until they weren't. Every police officer, no matter their division or title, was programmed to think that way.

He wondered why Aruba never told them about Trevion being in another relationship when they gave her notice of his death. And not just any relationship, but the only one that everybody seemed to know about, talk about, and admire. No one ever mentioned that he was involved with another woman. Was she his estranged wife? A bitter ex-wife? What was her real deal? Jayson wondered. There had to be a reason no one knew about Aruba. And had it not been for the detectives doing what they do during an

99

investigation, they wouldn't have known about her either.

Jayson pulled out the recording of Aruba's interview and pressed play, hoping to catch something that he might've overlooked before. The more he listened, the more he realized how full of shit she was, but it wasn't enough to say she was a murderer. He stopped the recording and started picking up the mess he made when the sight of Trevion and Bella together made his blood run cold.

"Mutherfuckerrrr!" He shouted.

He didn't know how he missed it before. But he figured he was so mad at Bella that the two plus two equaling four factor quickly escaped him. He let his emotions override his duties as a detective, and that's where he fucked up. When he really looked at the pictures, the puzzle pieces were starting to come together. It finally snapped. What were the odds that Bella was fucking Trevion and Aruba was his wife? This wasn't a coincidence. The two women had to be connected, or at best, knew each other. He was so excited that he now had a small something to work with. He jumped on his computer, entered his work credentials into the MPD database, and started searching Aruba's name, aliases, known affiliations, and anything that could tie her and Bella together.

"Oh, she likes the system, I see." He sneered, going through her file.

Although she had a lengthy record of her charges consisting of crimes, such as assault and battery, distribution of Class A, heroin to be exact, shoplifting, larceny, and possession of an illegal firearm, it was all the prostitution charges that stood out the most. And against his better judgment, he called Bella hoping to get some straight answers, but her phone was disconnected.

"Fuck!" He hollered. He looked at the police report, got Aruba's number, and called.

"You kill em, we chill em!" She jokingly answered.

"This is Detective Aveen from Miltton Homicide calling, looking to speak with Aruba Kingsley." He dryly said.

Surprised to hear who it was on the other end, she changed her tone. "Hello, Detective. How can I help you? Do you have some good news for me? She responded.

"Actually, I'm calling because I have some more questions for you that might help with the case. When would be a good time for you to come down to the station?"

'What they want to ask me?' She thought before answering. "Well, is it something I can answer over the phone?" She asked, trying to avoid any contact with the law.

"No, ma'am. We need a recorded statement."

"Fine." She sucked her teeth. "I can come tomorrow at ten in the morning."

"Great. I'll see you then."

Jayson sensed the attitude through the phone waves, but he was unmoved. He was bent on solving Trevion's murder, no matter what it took, even if it meant putting him in the crosshairs of being exposed.

CHAPTER 14:
ARUBA

Aruba, like Xandra, grew up in a fucked up situation. Only, she wasn't saved by a loving family like Xandra. The confines of the streets swallowed her up. She walked the same footpaths that her drug-addicted mother left for her to follow. By the age of fourteen, all she knew was selling ass for money and getting drugs to stay high, so she could sell more ass for more money. By the time she was twenty-five, she had run through more men and women than she could remember or put a number on.

She was a middle school dropout and not the brightest in the bunch, but she could read, do math, and write just enough to get her by. She made sure to know and understand the basics so that no one could ever play her out of the money that she worked so hard for. Or so she thought.

She had perfected the pussy selling business so well that she started recruiting bitches to work for her, giving her a chance to take a break from the real work. It was during those breaks she learned loyalty was nothing but a seven-letter word and was guaranteed by nobody.

Aruba was getting robbed left and right. All the money she accounted for and knew was coming her way was being pocketed by the hoes she hired. When it was time to pay up, they were never to be seen or heard from again. After taking as many shorts as she had, she realized no one, especially at her young age, took a woman seriously in that line of work; that's when Trevion came into the picture.

It wasn't hard for him to ease his way into the mind of the young, gullible Aruba and mold her into whatever he wanted her to be, and that's just what he did. Trevion loved the women who were broken, lost, desolate, timid, and naïve by every meaning of the word. It was a recipe for making them vulnerable, desperate, and solely dependent on him, just the way he liked it.

Aruba was everything he needed her to be; simpleminded, easy to take in, bleak, unresistant, and pretty. Her Espresso complexion was ravishing. It put many people in the mindset of the same radiance that graced the actress Lupita Nyongo. Her smile was bright, while her wide, round-shaped eyes captured the attention of anyone looking her way.

She had the typical cola-cola body shape that most men desired and looked for in women. And over the years, she maintained it all to keep an appearance for Trevion. He liked his hoes to look a certain kind of way, and she adhered to that ideology to the letter. But no matter what she did, how well she sucked him off or rode him into another dimension, she had no real win over Royelle and definitely not Bella.

With Royelle, Trevion quickly learned that those same cat-daddy tired-ass moves he used on other women weren't going to work on her. It didn't take him but a second to realize that her caliber of woman did not mimic Aruba's, and he needed to take a different approach. Royelle may have been green at times, but that's where the traits ended between her and the others.

With any of the other women he dealt with, all he had to do was keep his smooth appearances and jive talk going, take her out on a couple of dates, dick her down, add some pussy eating, clit licking, squirt, and orgasm cumming maneuvers, and he had her in the palms of his hand. With Royelle, none of that shit worked. He had to work to get her, and that's what he loved about her. She wasn't an easy catch like all the others. But when he got her; he got her.

Aruba wasn't too concerned with Royelle, though. She knew that

Royelle was nothing but a monetary gain for Trevion. At least that's what he told her. Bella, on the other hand, Aruba just couldn't stomach her. Trevion was set on her, and it killed Aruba to know it. She couldn't figure out why Bella was so special to Trevion. Was it the Italian and Latina in her? Was it the long, wavy Brown hair? Was it the natural Peach-shaped ass, the dimples in her cheeks, her smile, her Hazel eyes, or the way she deep throated him without a gag reflex the first time they had a threesome?

Was it the way she allowed him to fuck her without any push back like Aruba had done so many times when he wanted it anally? Was it the tricks she knew with Pop Rocks, Ice, and Peppermint while sucking him clean that kept him going after Bella time and time again? Aruba just didn't know, but her mind always wondered. And sadly, she never built up the courage to ask Trevion what Bella brought to the table that she didn't bring equally.

Often times she tried to step her game up in every area she lacked. Still, by the time she did, Bella had unintentionally done something better to grasp Trevion's attention even deeper, burning Aruba to her core. And now, with everything going on, she was intent on destroying Bella one way or another and didn't care what it was going to take to get it done.

Aruba paced her floors, anxious to know what questions Jayson might have for her. She was sure this was all Bella's fault. Everything was good until she stopped following the rules, and now Aruba was in a predicament.

She had the right mind to call Bella, invite her over, and whoop her ass the moment she walked through her door. Slapping Bella when she did made Aruba feel powerful. But if she could just beat the dog-shit out of her one good time, it would give her the satisfaction and payback she wanted for Bella stealing Trevion's attention away from her.

She blamed herself, though. Had she not done the six-year bid in Framingham's Women Prison for violating her probation, there would be no Royelle or Bella. She and Trevion were a great team, or so she thought. Had she been paying attention to all the signs, she would've seen that she was only valuable to him when it came to making runs, selling ass, and doing anything that was connected to the streets. When he didn't want his name tied to anything, he used Aruba. Trevion was a real piece of shit.

As she drove to the station, she tried to stay calm. She didn't want her attitude to be the reason the detectives might drill her harder, but it was difficult. The thought of Bella getting her caught up just wouldn't leave her. Since the whole situation with Trevion, she hadn't seen or heard from the police, and now, since Bella was caught on tape with him, things were getting sticky.

When the police initially questioned her, she played her part well. After all, she was Trevion's long-lost grieving wife. She had been gone for years, and when she got out, she wasn't in touch with him enough to know his business; that's what she told the police. There wasn't much that she could tell or offer them as far as information was concerned. And that was the same attitude she was going in with. She figured the less she spoke, the better. When she finally arrived at the station, Jayson was waiting for her in the front lobby.

"Good Morning, Mrs. Kingsley." He greeted.

"Call me Aruba." She spat.

She honestly did him a solid with her request. It was only out of respect, he called her Mrs. Kingsley, but he felt very uncomfortable doing so. There was something not right about the whole thing. It just didn't sit well with him.

He stood off to the side and waited for her to be cleared through the metal detectors. Once she was good, he swiped his badge, opened the door, and allowed her to walk in first. This was her second time at the station, and like Royelle, she absolutely hated the place. It gave her a slave mentality feeling. The vibe was always off, depressing, and it looked like it was meant to oppress people.

They each took their seat when they made it to the same small interrogation room Royelle was in when she got the news about Trevion. Aruba slouched in her chair, giving off the impression of someone who was bothered and didn't want to be in the same vicinity as the police.

"Where's your partner?" She asked, noting Detective Presley's absence.

"He hasn't made it in yet."

Jayson already knew Detective Presley wouldn't be in that early in the morning. He planned it that way. Detective Presley had a way of making potential witnesses go mute and disappear with his corny *I'm bigger and tougher than you* act, and Jayson didn't need that right now. He knew if Detective Presley wasn't present, he might have a better chance of getting the answers he needed.

"Anyway, can you tell me what was so important that we couldn't discuss it over the phone?"

Between Bella and having to go to the station, she just couldn't shake her fucked up attitude. The way she sat, spoke, and the annoying screwed-up face she wore was enough to make anyone want to slap her into kindness, but Jayson was unfazed.

"Well, there have been some developments in the case. So, any information you can provide will be helpful." He said, pressing the record button on his recorder.

"Developments? What kind of developments?"

Jayson stalled a bit before answering. He was already under the preconceived notion that Aruba would lie, so he wanted to give her a minute to gather her thoughts. This was a make-or-break move for him, so he had to play his hand the right way. He opened up his folder and pulled out the same pictures he showed Bella.

"Do you know who this is?"

He pointed at Bella and watched Aruba for any changes in her body language and facial expressions, but there were none. She maintained the same stale, turned-up, looking like she was smelling bad cheese face she had since she arrived. She already knew this was why he had called her down to the station in the first place, so mentally, she was prepared for it. Although the picture was dark, she knew that it was Bella. Anybody who knew Bella could tell it was her from miles away. Her voluminous hair and thick-fine body were hard for anyone to ignore or forget; even hating ass Aruba had to admit it.

"Am I supposed to know who that is?" She asked, looking back up at Jayson.

" I don't know. That's why we're here. To find out what you may or may not know. But that is your husband, correct?"

Aruba looked back down at the picture, acting as if she didn't see him in it before.

"Yea, that's him." She responded with an attitude.

"And you don't know who that woman is? Never seen or met her before?" He pressed.

Aruba sucked her teeth. " I already told you no."

"Well, do you know who's house they're at?"

Aruba looked back down at the picture, and nothing in the area looked familiar to her.

"No." She answered.

"Well, that's Trevion's house. The one he shared with her." Aruba's facial expressions slightly changed when she saw the picture of Royelle and Trevion appearing to be madly in love.

Two things were wrong. One, Aruba never knew about a house that Trevion had, let alone shared with Royelle. This was the first she was hearing about it. But it was clear from the way he was looking into her eyes and holding her in the picture; money wasn't the only thing Trevion was after when it came to Royelle. And two, if she didn't hate Bella before, she damn sure did now.

How was it that Bella knew about the house and she didn't? The only place she knew about was Trevion's small ass one-bedroom apartment that was near his construction site in Quincy. That place was restricted. No one was allowed there except for Trevion and his girls, and only with permission. He didn't like having all his women together in one place, so most times, it was just him and Aruba. It made her feel special knowing that it was just them two more often than not. But after seeing the size of the house he had with Royelle and knowing Bella not only knew about it but frequented it, suddenly had her feeling like she wasn't so extraordinary.

"Do you know her?" Jayson pointed at Royelle.

"I know of her. Why?" Aruba crossed her arms.

Aruba didn't realize it, but it was at this moment that she had just put Jayson completely on her radar. He knew he was somewhat on the right path, and although all the pieces still weren't connecting, he was getting warmer.

"What can you tell me about the relationship between her and your

107

husband?"

Jayson purposely avoided saying Trevion's name hoping that saying, '*your husband*' would piss her off enough knowing that Trevion had done her dirty. He was hoping it would cause her to spill the tea. Hurt people, hurt people, and that's what Jayson was gunning for.

"What is there to tell? They were fucking at one point, and that's it." She retorted.

"So, why didn't you tell us this before?"

Aruba swallowed the knot in her throat. She realized she had accidentally put herself inside of Charlotte's web. But she was quick on her feet.

"I didn't think there was anything to tell. They were fucking like most of the other women he fucked." She shot back, trying to calm the heat around her.

"What if I told you that they were doing more than just….fucking?"

"I would tell you that's a gawt damn lie." She said roughly.

"What if I told you I did some more digging and found this?"

Jayson slid Royelle and Trevion's marriage certificate across the table. Aruba sat straight up to look at it as the look of disgust accompanied her face.

"This is fake." She smirked.

"No, ma'am. I'm afraid it's not. It's a public record and can be found on the vital statistics website. I had no problem finding it. What I couldn't find was yours? When and where did you say you got married?" He asked trying to trip her up.

"I didn't. She snapped back. "Why would you need mines anyways? You saw what the hospital records said."

"Yes, but none of this marital information was available until now. So we have to ask everyone what their connection is to the deceased and ask for proof if necessary."

"Wait! Wait! Wait! Do you think one of us killed him?! Let me tell you something." She looked him straight in the eyes. "I had no reason to hurt that man, let alone kill him. You're barking up the wrong tree. I can't speak for them other bitches, but I damn sure can speak for me. And before you fix your lips to ask me anything else, I want a lawyer."

And just like that, the interview was over. Aruba wanted so badly to pull his card and tell him she knew about his connection to Bella because it was her escort service he called and used, but she had already denied knowing Bella. She didn't know much about politics or policing rules, but she was sure he could get into some kind of trouble for fucking a call girl. But then again, cops did so much shady shit, fucking a hoe was probably the least of I.A's worries.

CHAPTER 15:

TYING UP LOOSE ENDS

*I*t had been more than twenty-four hours since Adala's service, and Raymelle still hadn't walked through Royelle's door. Xandra didn't care. He needed time alone, and she understood that. Besides, it gave her and Raylina a chance to catch up on what Xandra had been missing. Although there wasn't much Raylina could offer, Xandra appreciated their time together. She hated to admit it, but she was missing all of them.

The death of Adala did not come easy for her. Being on the run was anything but fun. Even though she felt like no one could identify her and had nothing to run from, she needed time to clear her head after everything that went down. She didn't know how she would explain to Royelle that it was her that Trevion was in an exchange of gunfire with. Xandra knew Royelle would never understand it, no matter how she tried to explain it. So leaving abruptly for a while was the best thing she could think of.

Xandra looked around the house and found that not much had changed, other than everything related to Trevion being gone. Had it not been for the 8x10 wedding photo on Royelle's nightstand, no one would've known that a man once occupied the house at all. The only thing that gave the house a different feel was Royelle's absence. The house just didn't feel the same without her. No matter how square she may have been, she had a way of bringing joy to the house, and without her, the place was just quiet and dull.

Xandra walked around the house, contemplating whether to make breakfast or not when she came across one of the areas she knew had a camera set up. Despite her being M.I.A. for a while, she still wasn't in the clear. Like everybody else, she was a suspect and knew the police were probably checking out her background. The heat was still on for her and would be turned up to hell if she didn't make some moves quick. She needed the cameras Sion installed taken down immediately. Therefore, her first order of business was to get a hold of him.

'What's up, playa? What's the word on removing services from the old address? X.'

Xandra always spoke in code when dealing with certain kinds of business. It was her *just in case* way of thinking. It was a ploy to throw off the police and people who weren't supposed to know her moves. Typically, she wouldn't add a signature, but she had no choice in this case. It was a new phone and number, plus she had been gone for a bit. Without some kind of tag, Sion wouldn't have known it was her.

When Sion responded, he responded with curiosity. He had to be sure that who was texting him was exactly who he thought it to be. So rather than to go back and forth via text, he told Xandra that she needed a face-to-face appointment for termination of services. This was his way of validating who he was dealing with. They both agreed to 4 pm at their usual meeting spot.

It was rare for Sion to make an in-person appointment with people. And when he did, that meant you fucked up, or he needed to look you in the eye and get a feel for the shit you were bringing to the table. He could always tell the bullshitters from the go-getters by looking them in the eyes when they spoke. And if the vibe so was off, so wasn't any deal you thought you might have. As Xandra started walking towards the office, she paused when she heard keys jingling at the door.

"What's up, sis?" Raymelle spoke calmly.

"What's going on with you? You good?" She responded.

"I'm straight." He closed the door, locking it behind him. "Yo, my bad about yesterday, man. I was just in a real bad space, and you popping up like you did, didn't make things no better." He walked up to her and hugged her tightly.

"Damnnn! It's about fucking time, bro. You were acting like the Feds with your 21 questions and shit." She joked, hugging him back.

"Never that!" He shoved her head. "Come to the office right quick."

Raymelle walked into the office, Xandra followed behind. And even though she knew she was to blame for everyone's discord towards her. She was glad to see him in a better headspace.

"So, what's been up, bro?"

"What? Raylina didn't tell you?" He asked.

"I mean, she gave me bits and pieces, but y'all still treat her like a kid, so she ain't have much to say."

"Y'all?! You act like you ain't a part of, y'all!" He laughed. "But anyway, sis, this shit gets crazier by the fucking second."

"What'd you mean? Why?"

"I don't know what Raylina told you, but long story short, Trevion was shot and burned in his car, and the only way they could identify him was through dental records and his license plate."

"Wait?! What?! You fucking lying."

"I'm dead ass."

"That can't be true." She thought.

Xandra knew the possibility of him being shot was real, but being burned was not in the cards. She wondered if she might've hit some part of the tank that would cause it to catch fire when she was shooting at him. She remembered seeing a lot of smoke but never saw flames and didn't stick around to see if he was dead or alive. She had a hard time believing what she was hearing.

"Ok. Ok. Ok. Wait. Xandra scratched her head. "So, Trevion got shot and burned in his car? Did the police say where it happened or if they locked anyone up for it?" Xandra fished.

"Nah, they didn't. Charlyn said the D-Boys interrogated sis like she was the main suspect and that his wife was his next of kin."

"Well, we all know she ain't have shit to do with that," Xandra said.

Raymelle purposely threw that curveball about the other wife to see if Xandra would catch it. But she didn't, not right away anyways. It wasn't until a few minutes after that her light bulb switch turned on. Raymelle simpered and braced himself for her next reaction as he watched Xandra in her own head, trying to figure out if she heard what she thought she heard.

"Aye, bro. Who did you say identified him?" She needed to make sure she wasn't tripping.

"They say it was his wife. And her name ain't Royelle."

"Waittttt! Wait! Wait! Wait! Wait!" She shook her head as she loomed away from the desk. "Run that shit back, yo!"

Xandra reacted as he expected.

"You heard me, sis. That nigga got another fucking wife somewhere. They say she's the one that gave the de-tects his dental records."

"Nahhh, bro. You fucking with me, right?!" Xandra sneered.

"Come on, man. You know I don't play about shit like that. Especially when it comes to y'all."

Xandra couldn't believe what she was hearing. Not only was Trevion a lying, cheating, illegal side business, down-low, pimping, clown ass nigga. Now, piece of shit Polygamist can be added to the list of *'he ain't shit'* identifiers.

"Mannn, if that nigga wasn't already dead, I'd kill that pussy ass nigga myself," Xandra said, continuing to play her part.

"Shitttt. That makes two of us." Raymelle chimed in.

"On some real shit, bro; we didn't know a muthafucking thing about this scuzzball ass nigga?! Did they at least give Royelle the name of the trollop? Does anyone even know what she looks like? Where she lives?" Anything?" Xandra asked.

"I don't know none of that shit. Charlyn might, though."

Xandra wanted in on the other so-called wife. She wondered if the woman she saw with Trevion at the hotel was the same one calling herself his wife. She was determined to find out. The way Xandra saw it, the other woman was an added obstacle that needed to be eliminated A.S.A.P.

She looked at the time and realized she had thirty minutes to get back to the hood. When Sion gave a time and meeting place, yo ass had better been there. Time was money, and money wasn't anything Sion played about. Xandra let Raymelle know she needed to run a few errands and would link with him once she was done. They hugged and kissed each other on the cheek, and she was out.

She couldn't believe the level of traffic she was facing as she jumped onto the highway heading back to Dorchester. *'It's a fucking Saturday,'* she thought as she tried to maneuver through it. She weaved in and out of traffic until she finally decided to take the back streets and got off at the same Milton exit that Bella had used days prior. When she realized where she was, she quickly looked in the rearview mirror to make she wasn't being followed.

Naturally, she wouldn't have been so noided, but after the last episode of Trevion following her down that very same street, she felt like it was an obligation for her to check all her mirrors and make sure she was straight. No matter how secure she felt, she never left home without her gun, and today was no exception to that. She pulled her 45 from under her seat, took it off of safety, cocked it back, and placed it on her lap with her finger on the trigger.

She snickered a little as she thought about that fateful night that Trevion followed her. *'He really thought he had me,'* she thought as she slowly drove down Randolph Ave, heading into Milton. She took a lot of pleasure in knowing he was dead because of her, but it pained her at the same time, realizing what it cost her sister. Seeing Royelle laid up in the hospital bed before going to Adala's service did nothing but active Xandra's frenetic side. Per usual, if someone fucked with Royelle, they fucked with Xandra, and she would do whatever was necessary until further notice.

She slowly crept up to St. Michael's Parish and looked around at the ground as best she could. She was looking for anything that would resemble charred marks from a burning vehicle, and there was nothing. Before pulling over to the right, she checked her mirrors, making sure no one was following, put her car in park, gun in waist, and she stepped out, walking towards the area where the gun battle happened.

To her, it didn't matter how long ago the shit between her and Trevion happened, if he were burned in his car, there would be some evidence of a burning somewhere, like the detectives said. But as she looked around, she couldn't find one single thing that would signify anything happened there, let alone a car burning. Disappointed, she walked back to her truck and continued her journey to Sion. She wondered if maybe he got shot there and the car burned somewhere else. But, the story just didn't seem to fit.

Once there, she spotted him outside talking to some randoms she didn't know. She waited until he was done and the crowd was clear before stepping out of her truck. She walked into the small Tavern and spotted Sion at the bar as usual.

"About time. How long were you gonna sit there?" Sion asked while sipping his Hennesy on the rocks.

"You know I don't do strangers."

"Get her a double shot of Patron with a lime," Sion ordered his bartender.

They gave each other pounds, and Xandra sat down beside him. The mushy stuff, like hugs and kisses, was only reserved for the Blevins and not all of them either. Rayford would never have the pleasure of knowing how warm and loving Xandra's hugs actually were.

"So let's get to it. You know my motto—"

"Yea. Yea. Time is money. I know Sion." Xandra rolled her eyes.

"So, what's up? You need services removed. Why?"

"Come on, Sion. You smart. Ain't it obvious. Homeboy is dead. If the police decide to search her crib and find those cameras, it's gonna link back to you and me. Why else would I want them taken out?"

"Nah, love. It wouldn't link back to me. I make sure none of our shit is connected to my services in any way. Now would it link back to you, probably? But you haven't told anyone about it, so you good."

Xandra wanted to bust him in his lip. She wasn't in the mood and didn't need all the sarcasm or smart-mouth shit he was spitting at her. All she needed him to do was the job she came to pay him for.

"So, how much is it gonna cost?"

"That ain't shit to remove. I got chu on that one. All I need is the time and day. And don't pull that shit you did last time. Make sure that the time you give me is the time that's gonna work, and we ain't gotta kill no one cause you fucked up on timing. And none of that same day shit either."

" A'ight! Damn! Relax! I got you! Give me a few days, and I'll holla at you."

Xandra went into her bag, pulled out $500, and placed it on top of the bar. "No job I need done goes without payment. Especially when the job is for tying up loose ends."

Sion picked up the money, looked at it, and then back at Xandra.

"Aye yo, let me ask you something." He said.

"What's that?"

"Where the fuck you been? Why I ain't seen or heard from you?"

"Why? You been looking for me?" She said seductively.

"Nah, I haven't. But you know the streets talk. Said you been missing since old boy got popped. What you got to do with that?" He looked her dead in the eyes.

"I ain't got shit to do with that. I wasn't even here when it happened. I mean, I never liked the nigga, but I ain't got shit to do with that." She said with a straight face.

"Ayeee." Sion threw his hands up. "Those can of sardines ain't for me to eat. Ya dig."

"Or me! What chu mean?" Xandra giggled.

"A'ight lil mama. I was just asking."

"I hear you. But I'm good. Clean."

Xandra picked up her shot glass, threw back the double shot of Patron, slammed the glass down, and walked out. Sion couldn't tell if she was lying or not, but he knew street code. A secret revealed is a secret you die for.

CHAPTER 16:
DOING TOO MUCH

*S*ince Xandra's return, she made it her business to visit Royelle every morning before the 7 a.m. shift change. As much as she hated being there that early, it was the only way she could avoid crowds and running into Rayford, who was one smart-ass comment away from being punched in the throat. Everyone always tried to justify his behaviors, saying that's who he was, but Xandra was never in the business of pacifying his fucked up ways. The respect he gave her, she gave in return. He didn't care for her, and likewise, she despised him.

Every visit Xandra had with Royelle was routine. She got in the room, kissed her on the forehead, grabbed her right hand, and whispered, *'Get up bitch. We got shit to do, and I don't wanna do it alone. No Salt.'* She didn't know if Royelle could hear her or not, but she was determined to let Royelle know that she was there and anxiously waiting for her to wake up.

Although she made her visits frequent, she hated the guilt that followed. Each visit reminded her that had it not been for the shit she did, Royelle wouldn't be in the predicament she was in, and she was fixated on making it right. Xandra wasn't going to let what happened to Royelle be for nothing. The truth about Trevion had to come out, and it could only come from her.

She mapped out how she would handle the police if they got to questioning her for any reason, but what she didn't plan for was a dead Trevion that was shot and burned. That information was new and forced her to change her whole game plan. Now it involved her doing research that she wasn't prepared to do.

Something about Trevion's death just didn't sit well with her. Every time she tried to shake the uneasy feeling off, an offbeat level of anxiety came over her. She knew she was a pretty good shot and was certain she didn't touch his car. She had to get to the bottom of the details of where he was found, how he was burned, and what coroner's office was in charge, only she had no idea where to start. But she wasn't going to be satisfied until she knew for sure that the damage she did matched the rumors on the street. But before she could make any more moves, she had to get the cameras out of the house.

After clocking Raymelle and Raylina's movements closely, she knew the best time for Sion to come was at 9:30 any morning. With that in mind, she called Sion with the hopes of meeting him at Royelle's the following day.

"What it do?" He answered after the second ring.

"A'int shit. What's the deal for tomorrow? She asked.

Sion thought about it for a second before responding. "Can I just come today?" He asked.

Xandra sucked her teeth. "Nigga, wasn't it you who said I couldn't do same-day shit?!"

"Man, don't worry about it. Just answer the fucking question." He laughed off.

This moment felt like Deju Vu for Xandra, and she was in no joking mood. She wanted done what needed to be done, and that's it. Had she known Sion was gonna flip a same-day service on her, she would've been more prepared. She told Sion she'd call him back after checking on Raymelle and Raylina's movements. *'This nigga make me sick.'* She thought while dialing Raymelle.

"Hey sis, what's up," he answered.

"A'int shit. On my way over there. Y'all want something to eat?"

"Nah, sis. We ain't even home. We bout to pick Pops up and head to the hospital. You should come with us."

Raymelle had no idea that Xandra had visited Royelle religiously every morning, and that's just the way she wanted to keep it.

"Nah, bro, y'all go. You know me and the hospitals don't vibe. Kiss her for me and tell her I love her."

"On dawgs, sis, you gotta break out of that habit."

"You know I can't see her like that. It was the same thing with momma; you know that."

After a few back and forth exchanges with Raymelle, Xandra hung up the phone, called Sion, and let him know she would meet him at Royelle's in twenty.

By the time Raymelle pulled up on the Loma, Rayford was looking sharp and already sitting on the porch waiting on him. Outside of Adala's funeral, this was the first time he and Raylina had seen their father looking that way in a very long time, and it piqued Raymelle's interest. Rayford was clean and stylish in a Wine collared shirt, Beige slacks, Wine shoes, and a Wine handkerchief sticking out of his left shirt pocket. When he got in the car, he smelled like a mixture of Men's soap and Old Spice cologne. Even though his scent was strong, Raymelle was impressed.

"Where you going, cat daddy?" Raymelle joked.

"Yuh like? Mi a guh si mi dawta." Rayford smiled.

"I mean, it's about damn time no one gotta tell you to do something with yourself. You sure you ain't got no girlfriend up in that house or lingering around somewhere?" Raymelle chuckled.

Rayford sucked his teeth and slapped Raymelle upside the head.

"Watch your mouth bwoy. Yuh madda nuh bin dead ah month yet, an yuh speaking blasphemy."

"Pops, I'm just joking, damn."

Getting to the hospital from The Blevins house was a hop, skip, and jump. But sometimes, with the traffic on Blue Hill Ave and Dudley Street, what should be a five to six-minute drive can sometimes turn into fifteen easy. Raylina, however, was relieved when they finally made it. She was tired of the two of them going back and forth about Rayford's appearance

119

and a potential new girlfriend. She didn't give two-shits about his appearance, and she was definitely on Raymelle's side when it came to the girlfriend thing. If there was one, she would never be accepted as far as they were concerned.

"So, where's what's her name today? Why isn't she here?" Rayford clowned, walking towards the hospital elevators.

"Man, Pops, I don't know and don't start. And why you so pressed about her anyway?"

"Pressed? What's pressed?" He tried to understand the slang.

"Nothing Pops. Leave it alone. It ain't nine in the damn morning, and you already with the shits."

Rayford chuckled. " I was just want to know why she's not here?"

"Pops! That's enough, man! Every day since Royelle got to the hospital, all you've been talking about is Xandra this, Xandra that. Nobody gives a fuck about that right now. Focus on your daughter, man. Your daughter!"

"Yeh Yeh." Rayford waved Raymelle off and pressed the ICU's intercom button to get the attention of the nurses sitting at the nurse's station.

In no way was Raymelle trying to take away from how much Xandra meant to him and the others; he was just sick of Rayford's mouth. He knew Rayford couldn't stand her, and seeing how she had been missing in action, did nothing but allow Rayford the opportunity to try and convince others that she wasn't shit; it never worked.

"Good morning. How can I help you?" The nurse asked through the intercom.

"Good Morning. We're here for Royelle Kingsley," Raymelle answered.

"Come on in." The nurse buzzed the automatic doors.

By the time they got to Royelle's room, they could tell that the nurses had been on their shit. As usual, Royelle's face was washed, hair brushed, her johnny and underneath her nails were clean, her catheter bag was emptied, and her IV bags were all replaced. They made sure the Blevins never had a reason to complain.

"Hey, sis." Raylina softly whispered.

It made her smile to see her sister looking better every day. She wasn't 100% herself, but she wasn't the 20% she was when she first got there. Raylina pulled out her phone and started taking pictures.

"Wah yuh ah duh?" Rayford snapped.

"I'm taking pictures, daddy." She frowned, continuing to take photos.

"Mi cya si dat? Mi wa fi kno why?"

"Pops, chill. Since day one, she's been doing that so Royelle can see what she came from when she wakes up. You'd know that if you were here with us every day."

Rayford was always looking for a target to bully. Since he couldn't do it with Raymelle and Royelle wasn't at his disposal, he chose Raylina. Knowing her brother had her back, Raylina wasn't concerned with Rayford's misery. She stayed out of the conversation and focused on her sister.

"Sis, you have to come out of this. Wake up, girl." Raylina gently stroked Royelle's hair.

Finding words was always hard for Raymelle, so he just looked on. Rayford was Rayford. No emotions, no words, no nothing, just there. Nobody ever knew what he was thinking or feeling. They just knew he was there.

"You know, now that she's back, the least she can do is visit or call."

"Pops! You still on that shit? What does Xandra not being here gotta do with us?! We're here! And that's all that matters."

Rayford's obsession with Xandra being back was annoying the fuck out of Raymelle. Not seeing her or knowing her movements seemed to grip Rayford by the balls. It was all he talked about since her return, and it was sickening.

"Mi jus a seh. Luk at har." He pointed at Royelle. "You would think her friend would be here for her."

"Pops! You're doing way too much! I swear. If you keep on with this shit, I'm gonna ban you from coming up here myself. Don't—"

Before Raymelle could finish his complete thought, Rayford grabbed him by the collar and threw him up against the wall.

"Mi gwine tell yuh sinting bwoy! I'm your father, you're not mines! You're gonna watch how you talk to me. Yuh undastan?!

"Man, get the fuck off of me!" Raymelle said through his clenched-down teeth. He grabbed his fathers' hands and pushed them off of him. "Every time you come around here, you with some bullshit. You be doing too much! Why the fuck can't you stay focused on her?! Your daughter! You got some shit with you, man. It's no wonder you and Royelle can't fucking get along."

"Yuh nuh kno shit bowy! Wi cyaa get along cuz of yuh mada! She was the problem between us. She pinned both of your sisters against me!"

"Daddy, please." Raylina softly spoke, hoping he would calm down.

"Mind yuh biznizz licckle gyal! Yuh nuh innocent eena any ah dis!" He snapped.

With all the commotion going on, no one had noticed that Royelle started making subtle movements. And between all the utters, suddenly the sounds of her machines began blaring, getting everyone's attention. They all froze as the first nurse came rushing into the room. When she saw all the machines flashing red and Royelle's vitals through the roof, she yelled out to the nurse's station, "Somebody page the doctors! Sorry! But you guys are gonna have to go to the family room, now!" The nurse directed.

"Man, what's going on?!" Raymelle yelled.

"Please! You all have to leave the room now!" She repeated as all the other nurses rushed in.

Raymelle had no level of understanding. Rayford was looking as dumb as he always had, and Raylina looked worried and lost, but she stayed focused. She quickly called Charlyn, gave her the 411, and tried calling Xandra to do the same, but she didn't answer.

Xandra saw Raylina calling, but she ignored the calls when she saw that Sion was at the tail end of gathering all his shit. She wanted to be sure he was out of the house long gone before calling Raylina back. But Raylina was relentless. Now that she knew Xandra was back and had a way to reach her, she was stopping at nothing to get in touch with her. She called back to back until Xandra finally answered.

"Girlllll! You better be fucking dying right now with the way you blowing my shit up."

"Sissss! Something is happening with Royelle!" She cried into the phone.

"What?! What the fuck are you talking about?! What's happening?!"

"I don't know, sis. They kicked us out of the room."

"I'll be there!" Xandra hung up and walked into the hallway, where she found Sion and his boys looking suspicious at the front door.

"Everything good?" Sion asked.

"I don't know. But I gotta go. Y'all done?"

"We good. But your outside ain't."

"Fuck you talking about?" Xandra walked to the family room and peeked out the blinds.

"The fuck." She walked back out to where Sion was at. "I don't know what the fuck that's about, but y'all good. Y'all got cable uniforms on."

"Man, that's beside the point. These mutha fuckers is watching this house for a reason."

"A'ight. Hold on." She rolled her eyes.

This was not the shit she needed right now. She was trying to get to her sister, and Sion being paranoid about leaving the house prolonged the situation. She huffed as she walked outside and towards the D-Boy's car while Sion peeked out the blinds.

"How's it going, detectives?" Xandra smiled.

"How are you?" Detective Presley replied.

"I'm good. Thank you. My sister isn't here, but is there something I can help you, gentlemen, with?" She politely asked.

"Sister? We weren't aware that Mrs. Blevins had a sister." Detective Presley said.

Xandra noticed Detective Presley calling Royelle by her maiden name. She wanted to correct him but left well enough.

"What's your name?" Detective Presley continued.

"Muneca."

"I'm Detective Presley. This is my partner, Detective Aveen.

Xandra stuck her hand out to shake both of theirs as Sion continued to look on, wondering what the fuck it was that she was doing. Detective

Aveen hadn't said a word the whole time. He only observed and took mental notes of her calmness and pleasant demeanor.

"Well, was there something you guys needed? Water, soda, juice, tea?" She clowned.

"No. We're just canvassing the area."

"Canvassing? From in front of my sister's house? Didn't the murder happen down the street?"

Instantly she fomented their interest. She was doing too much without realizing it.

"Murder down the street? We're not talking about that murder." Detective Presley said.

"Ohhh!" She acted surprised. "You're here about her husband Trevion? I understand now. Well, for sure, I cant help with that. But I damn sure hope y'all find out who did it."

"We're working on it." Detective Presley responded.

"Well, thank you. When my sister wakes up, I'm sure she'll be happy to hear that.

"How is she? Your sister?" Detective Presley snidely asked.

"She's getting better."

"Glad to hear it. Well, we'll check back from time to time. Here are our cards in case anything comes up that you think might be helpful to the case."

Detective Presley reached into the cup holder, grabbed he and Detective Aveen's business cards, and handed them to her.

"Not a problem, sir. You guys have a great day. Don't work too hard, huh."

"Always." Detective Presley shot back.

"Pig Muthafuckers," she mumbled under her breath as she walked back into the house to a concerned Sion.

"Did you take notes of that, Jayson," Thomas asked?

"Of course I did."

"Good. Cause there's something about that one there." Detective Presley said.

Something about her struck his interest; he just couldn't quite put his finger on it. But he had a strong gut feeling about her.

"X! What the fuck was you doing?" Sion asked.

"Investigating them while they were investigating us. Fuck you think I was doing. Every dog has a pattern, even the specially trained ones."

CHAPTER 17:
AWAKE

ime appears to tick away slower than usual when your energy is spent. It had been nearly two hours since they were kicked out of Royelle's room, but to them, it felt like twenty-four. No one had come to them with an update, and with every passing second that they failed to report, more agitation emerged around them. Even Charlyn, the most rational one of the group, grew impatient but remained reserved in an effort to keep the others calm.

Raymelle was a ticking time bomb. He wanted to beat his father senselessly. The way Raymelle saw it, the only reason shit was happening the way it was, was because of his fathers' bullshit. Everything, no matter the situation, good, bad, or in-between, if Rayford showed up, those situations turned from sugar to shit in a hot-milli second. And Raymelle was sick of it. If something bad came out of this situation with Royelle, Rayford minus-well had better start preparing for his own funeral.

As a result, she struck up stupid conversations about the shit happening on the news, sports, things Royelle did for her at work, at the courthouses, and joked about how much she teased Royelle on becoming an attorney with her own office someday. She did all she could to lighten the load and try to keep their minds on everything except the amount of time they've been waiting to hear about Royelle. It was a failed effort.

While they pretended to listen, Raylina continued to scroll through social media. Rayford, while looking directly at Charlyn, was never quite listening. He really wanted her to shut the fuck up. The sounds of a woman going on and on irked him to the fullest. But he knew his place when he was up against powerful women. To evade Rayford from causing a scene, Xandra sat on the floor outside the waiting room, creating timelines on her phone of all the shit that had been transpiring from day one. The goal was to give it to Royelle when she was ready.

Raymelle was in his head trying to piece together who Trevion really was and why someone wanted him dead. But, Royelle and Trevion had always been private about their relationship. It wasn't until now that Raymelle realized he didn't know shit about the relationship like he once thought. All he knew was that Trevion owned a construction and roofing company, had no kids, very little to no family or friends, and was dumb-struck crazy about Royelle. But, outside of that, Raymelle was clueless when it came to Trevion, giving him more fuel to be mad at himself for letting his sister down.

He thought about all the times he and Trevion hung out over the years, and he couldn't think of a single time that he had ever needed to question Trevion's loyalty to Royelle or her family. And it had him feeling fucked up because of it. As a man, he felt it was his duty to pick up on Trevion's type of bullshit and protect his sisters from it. Feeling like he didn't do his part made him feel less of a man. The guilt trip was weighing heavy. Above and beyond that, his sister was going through heavy shit, and there wasn't a thing he could do about it except wait.

"Wah gwan man. Why are these people taking so long?" Rayford asked.

"I don't know. But I'm about to go find out." Raymelle answered.

As soon as he headed out of the room in the direction to the nurses' station, he spotted Dr. Pisces, Dr. Schwartz, and two nurses walking towards his direction. Xandra waited for them to go inside and followed behind, disregarding Rayford's irritancy of her presence.

"Hello, folks." Dr. Pisces greeted. "Would you all like to talk here or in the conference room?"

"We can talk here. It's just us." Raymelle anxiously replied.

Xandra moved over to the furthest side away from Rayford, and Raylina followed, wrapping her left arm around Xandra's back. Xandra reciprocated the gesture with her right arm across Raylina's shoulders. And just like that, Raylina felt more safe and secure. If bad news was coming, at least she had Xandra to help her through it.

"First, I am sorry to keep you all waiting. In these situations, it's always best that the family waits outside of the room so that the medical team can work effectively and efficiently. Second. The good news is Royelle is awake."

The room that was entirely clouded with confusion, anger, fear, and worries was now released from its death grip. It felt like a dark cloudy day had just been conquered by the sun. The sighs of relief covered the room.

"I know it's fantastic news, but there is still a lot we need to talk about." Dr. Pisces said.

"Ok," Raymelle responded skeptically.

"We took the tube out of her mouth; however, she is still connected to everything else. She is very, very tired, and we are waiting on some additional test results that we requested. I will let the Neurologist Dr. Schwartz explain from here."

Everyone turned their attention to him, anticipating his remarks.

"I am happy to say that the images showed no signs of severe trauma to the brain, which wasn't much of a surprise to us. There isn't any bleeding, swelling, or clots in or around the brain either. However, she has shaken it up a bit from the impact, causing her to become fuzzy and off-balance. For the most part, as far as any visible injury is concerned, there is nothing. Also, all of her blood tests came back normal as well."

"Doc? I feel like more is coming, but not in a good way. So, say what you gotta say." Raymelle snapped.

Charlyn gently rubbed his back as a way of saying calm down without actually saying it.

"This may be premature, but we believe that Royelle may have suffered

128

some damage to her frontal lobe where her short-term memory is stored."

"What does that mean?." Raymelle asked.

Everyone but Charlyn stood by quietly waiting on the response. She needed clarity.

"But you said it was too premature to tell. So, does that mean we're just waiting for something else to come back?" Charlyn questioned.

"Premature in the sense that we asked basic household questions, such as; What's your name? "Where do you live? Do you know why you're here? What's the last thing you remember doing? She was only able to answer a few of those questions. If we are right in our assessments, Royelle may be suffering from what we call Dissociative Amnesia." Dr. Schwartz said.

"Dis-ah-what?" Raymelle frowned.

"Dissociative Amnesia. While there are several types of Dissociative Amnesia, we believe Royelle may be suffering from Systematized Amnesia. To put it in easier terms, situational amnesia."

"What's that?" Xandra quickly asked.

"Systematized amnesia is a loss of memories related to a specific category or individual. For example, someone may forget all of their memories involving a particular person or time in their life. In Royelle's case, based on what we've asked her so far, it seems that she can only remember the things that are unrelated to the accident."

"But the only way for us to know for sure is to ask more questions with all of you present. We'd like to see how she responds to the people she knows and the questions we ask. But we ask that you please keep an open mind and stay calm. She's scared, tired, and still trying to process what's going on around her." Dr. Schwartz continued.

Everyone was at a loss. They weren't sure what to make of the news and wondered what kind of Royelle they would be standing in front of. Was she going to be a confused Alzheimer's type of patient like Adala, or a two-second talking Tom, like the dude in the movie First 50 Dates? Everyone was anxious to know.

"Can we go to her now?" Raymelle asked.

"Let's go." Dr. Pisces smiled and opened the door for the family to leave out first.

Raymelle, Xandra, and Raylina wanted to run down the hall into her room, but they respected what the doctor said. Not to mention, they had no idea what they were about to walk into. Raymelle walked in first, followed by his two sisters and Charlyn. Rayford stayed outside of the room.

"What's up, sis. How you feeling?" Raymelle smiled big.

"Raymelle?" Her voice cracked.

"Yea, man." Raymelle replied, trying not to cry.

He was so excited to hear her say his name. *'She might have amnesia, but she damn sure remember me.'* He thought. Equally, Royelle was excited to see her siblings. It made this moment of confusion a little more sustainable to handle. But now, she had questions.

"Why am I in the hospital?" She asked.

Hesitantly Raymelle answered. "You were in a car accident."

"Accident? When?" She mustered up the strength to ask.

"Don't worry about that. What matters now is you getting better." Xandra responded.

The three made their way to the foot of the bed as the doctors approached Royelle's bedside. And although Xandra's guilt made her feel like her chest was caving in from suffocation, she was happy to see Royelle up and talking.

"Royelle, I'm going to check your vitals again. Is that ok?" Dr. Pisces asked.

Royelle nodded up and down while everyone else in the room remained quiet, watching the doctor do her thing.

Everything sounds good." Dr. Pisces smiled.

When Royelle finally noticed Charlyn, she was surprised.

"Charlyn?"

"Yes, I'm here, darling. Been here." She smiled with tears in her eyes.

"I never saw you come you in."

Royelle attempted to scoot herself up in the bed when she felt a slight pullback, something she hadn't noticed or felt when she first woke up. She looked down at her wrists and saw restraints. When she couldn't release them from the grasp they were in, she looked up at Raymelle and began to panic.

"Brother? Why am I tied down?" She asked nervously.

"Just to make sure you're ok, sis."

"Ok? Ok, from what?"

She frantically looked at everyone in the room, trying endlessly to remove the restraints as worriedness clouded her beautiful facial features. Her face scrunched up, her eyebrows compressed together, forming a v-like shape, and her eyes drooped, looking like Autumn leaves and flowers when they begin to wilt due to the season change.

"What is going on," She questioned.

With her wrist and ankles bound, she jerked up and down and side to side, looking like Emily Rose when she was having an exorcism performed. She screamed feverishly at those around her as they watched the doctors try to calm her down. None of them liked seeing her look like a caged animal, but it was for her own good.

"Royelle, we need you to calm down," Dr. Pisces said.

"Get these things off of me!" She yelled.

"I will. But first, I need you to calm down."

"Why do I have these on?!"

"I will tell you the minute you calm down."

"Tell me nowww!" Royelle cried.

"Mrs. Kingsley, I need for you to calm down first."

"Don't tell me to calm down!"

"I'm going to ask you one more time."

"Fuck you!" Royelle hollered.

"Royelle!" Raymelle yelled. It was the first time he had ever heard her use that kind of language. "Chill out man."

"Get these off of me!" Royelle stared at the doctor with flames in her eyes never acknowledging Raymelle.

"Nurse. Lorazepam. 5cc, please. Right away!" Dr. Pisces ordered the nurse to get her the sedation medication.

"Doctor, please. Give us a minute. Let me try something before you do that," Charlyn pleaded.

"One-shot. If it doesn't work, we will have to sedate her."

Charlyn walked over to where the doctor was standing and bent down at eye level with Royelle giving her the look a Lioness gives her cubs when she's trying to tame them.

"Royelle, look at me, and you better listen. If you don't get your ass under control, they will give you some of that medicine, and you will be here longer than you want to be. The sooner they can talk to you and run some more tests without you being belligerent, the closer to going home you'll be. I understand not knowing what's going on is scary for you, but if you don't pull yourself together, you won't find out."

Charlyn's face was like steel, cold with no movement, and her eyes had a stoic blaze to them, further letting Royelle know that Charlyn wasn't playing with her. Royelle gave her the same look in return, but she backed down when she saw Charlyn wasn't digressing.

"Fine." She responded, sounding like a five-year-old having a tantrum.

She turned her head away from Charlyn, knowing better than to disrespect her in any form or fashion. She was much like a mother figure to her, and when she spoke to Royelle as she did, it reminded her of the way Adala used to talk to her when she was younger. Noticing the calm that Charlyn was able to place upon Royelle, Dr. Pisces took the opportunity to approach Royelle's bedside again.

Xandra remained in the back, still quiet, smiling a bit as she watched and listened to Charlyn do her thing. She gave Xandra the same feeling it gave Royelle; a sense of an authority figure, a momma bear type of woman, and Xandra admired that. Raymelle and Raylina simply watched Charlyn take control as she did in previous situations. Meanwhile, good for nothing Rayford continued to stand outside of Royelle's door, listening to all the commotion inside the room. He was more concerned with learning about her level of amnesia and how he could use it to his advantage than he was about her overall health condition; that was the least of his concerns.

"Can you take these off of me? I'm calm now." Royelle softly asked.

"No. Not yet. But I promise we will take them off soon."

Royelle turned her head in the opposite direction again and closed her eyes. She wanted to cuss everyone out for the way the Dr's were treating her and the lack of defense she was getting from her family. But she knew one false move meant her going night-night nigga at least until the next day.

"Royelle. Dr. Schwartz and I need to ask you some questions. Can you please turn towards us so that we can hear your responses clearly?" Dr. Pisces asked.

They waited a couple of minutes to see if she would comply, and she did. She attempted to sit up again, but the restraints didn't allow the capacity. Royelle huffed at the feeling.

"It's ok. We'll get those off you in just a minute." Dr. Pisces reassured. "Now, some of these questions may sound silly, but we have to ask them, ok."

Royelle nodded her head yes.

"What's your full name?" Dr. Schwartz asked.

"Royelle Blevins."

Everyone, the doctors included, already knew that was strike one.

"How old are you?"

"29 soon to be 30."

"Do you know where you are?"

"The hospital."

"Which one?"

"Boston Medical Center, right? That's what that board says." Royelle pointed at the whiteboard hung on the wall in front of her.

"Do you have any children or pets?"

"No children and I have a dog named Chasity."

"Do you know your phone number?"

"Yes. 617-213-8546"

"What are the names of your parents?"

"Adala and Rayford Blevins."

"Who are these people?" Dr. Schwartz pointed around the room. "What's their names and their relation to you."

"That's my brother Raymelle and my sisters Raylina and Xandra."

"And she?" Dr. Schwartz pointed at Charlyn.

"She's like a second mother to me and my boss, Charlyn."

"Ok. Wonderful. That's long-term." Dr. Schwartz said, looking at the nurse who was taking notes. "Now tell me about the day you arrived here."

Royelle paused for a minute, trying to recollect the day's events, but she kept drawing a blank. She closed her eyes to see if that would help, but everything was pitch black. And for someone so cold-hearted all the time, Xandra couldn't help the emotions she felt as she released a few tears listening and watching her sister go through the motions.

"I'm not sure. I honestly can't remember."

"Do you know why you're here?"

"No."

Everyone was baffled. Raymelle had told her why she was there just two minutes before that.

"Are you married?"

Royelle chuckled. "Oh! No, sir."

"Ever been married?"

"No, sir."

"Boyfriend? Any guy you might be seeing?"

Royelle laughed louder. "No, sir."

"Ok. I think I have all that I need."

"Am I ok?" Royelle curiously asked.

"Yes. You are ok, but your brain is still a bit jolted from the car accident that brought you here."

Royelle paused.

"Car accident? I was in a car accident?" She questioned.

"Yes, you were."

"When?"

"Almost four weeks ago."

"Four weeks! I've been here for a month?!" Royelle got more excited.

"Yes. But you are doing well. Your body and brain just needed much rest after the impact."

After giving her that information, the doctors observed Royelle for a moment before deciding what to do next. When they noted her calm demeanor, they decided to remove the restraints. And once the restrictions were gone, Royelle released a deep moan as she sat up.

"Ok, doctor. What's really wrong with me? Just tell me, please." She pleaded.

"You have what we believe to be Dissociative Amnesia. The way you answered your questions shows your long-term memory is fine, but anything surrounding the accident is a blur." Dr. Schwartz minced his words.

"I'm sorry. I have what?"

Dr. Schwartz figured the best way to answer it for her was to give her the same explanation he had given her family minutes earlier. Royelle's eyebrows frowned as she heavily gasped. She was confused. It was a lot of information for someone who had just woke up from a coma to take in. She couldn't understand how she went to sleep one way and woke up another. Things like that simply didn't happen to her.

"How long will I be like this?" She whimpered.

"Honestly, it could be a matter of hours, days, weeks, maybe even years. It's tough to tell with each case. However, what we know about Dissociative Amnesia is that with great therapy, things will gradually start coming back to you in phases, spurts, and even in big productions. Your memory isn't gone forever, and we have people who can try to help you get it back."

Royelle was riddled with sadness.

"Doc, how can we help her in the meantime?" Raymelle asked.

"There are several things you can do. For starters, she will need a lot of rest; that includes no working." The doctor looked over at Charlyn.

"That goes without saying." Charlyn shot back.

"She'll need someone around her at all times until she is completely settled on her feet and able to function without being reminded."

"Can I go home?" Royelle asked.

"Not today. We want to observe your progress for a few more days, at which time we can discuss your discharge plans.

Royelle wanted to go off but knew the doctors would put her down like a dog without hesitation. To avoid giving them the pleasure, she turned her head and let her tears fall wherever they landed. She had nothing left to give anyone in the room.

"Do you all have any more questions for us before we go?" Dr. Pisces asked.

"No." They all replied in unison.

135

"Royelle?" Dr. Pisces looked over at her.

"I just wanna go home." Royelle sadly said.

"Of course. And we will get you there. We just want to make sure we don't do it ill-advisedly."

"Thank you, Dr.'s. We appreciate all of you." Charlyn said as the doctors left the room.

"Sis, we're here. We got you." Raymelle reminded.

For the next several hours, they stayed in the room with her, watching as the nurses came in and out every so often, checking her vitals, IV bags and giving her medicine that would eventually put her out. Rayford, who never stepped foot into the room, could hear everything that was going on. He was surrounded in joy at the fact that his daughter was up, alive, and still not 100% herself. This reassured him that she wouldn't be able to fight for Power of Attorney, still deeming him the only one with authority over everything surrounding Adala.

CHAPTER 18:
HOME SWEET HOME

*F*our weeks laying dormant in a hospital bed requires more than just opening your eyes. The few days that Dr. Pisces promised her to be in the hospital turned into a few weeks. Royelle had to learn to walk again, feed herself, shower herself, and wipe herself after every bathroom run. The idea of needing to depend on others like she was an elderly patient would not work for her. She was determined to get it all back, and she did.

Leading up to the day of Royelle going home, everyone was preparing for her arrival and today was no different. The idea was to try and create a sense of normalcy for her. Therefore, Raylina and Xandra made sure her house was as clean as she always had it, and it smelled just the way she liked it, with the scent of her favorite Pure Energy and Peace candles filling the air.

Xandra often contemplated removing the wedding picture out of Royelle's room but finally decided against it. She needed Royelle to remember Trevion in the worst way. She figured if Royelle could remember him, it would make revealing who he really was much easier to do. So, she left the picture on the nightstand and stuck her middle finger up at him as she walked out of the room.

Raymelle walked into the house, taken aback by how good it looked and smelled. It wasn't that the house was dirty; it just didn't have the Royelle effect to it. "All right, Molly the Maids! Look at y'all go!" He joked, walking towards the kitchen. As usual, like any other big brother, he was a big pain in the ass, who never lifted a finger to clean even as kids. They ignored his comment and continued to finish what they were doing.

"Which one of y'all riding with me to go get, sis?"

Raylina jumped in and volunteered before Xandra could say anything. She didn't care though. She wasn't going anyways. She had another agenda in mind. Raylina quickly finished up what she was doing, jumped in the shower, got dressed, and thirty minutes later, she and Raymelle were out the door. Once the coast was clear, Xandra went into Trevion's office to execute her next exploration. From the exchange she had with the D-Boys in front of Royelle's house, she knew they were about to look into her or already had. She didn't know why no one had questioned her about Benton's murder yet when she was sure Benton was recording everything that fateful day. The only thing that made sense to her was that Trevion must've done something to the recording device before she made it to the porch. Either way, she vowed to stay out of the way of anything moving. Keeping a low profile and staying out of the way was critical at this point.

Since she was sure that the detectives were more than likely going to investigate her, she felt it was fitting for her to reciprocate the gesture. Of all the crooked shit that Sion had taught her in the past, researching people was the one thing she truly perfected. It was like stealing candy from a baby. She googled every public profile search engine she could think of, even the ones that scamming ass Sion had given her access to. She grabbed the business cards Detective Presley gave her and, one by one, began to search and create portfolios on each of them, no matter how minuscule the information. It took a bit of time, but she secured their addresses, possible relatives, and their locations. Xandra was cold with it. And because Google and social media were a muthafucker, it was easy for her to access the images of both detectives. She was determined to learn every and anything she could about them, *just in case.*

Although overjoyed with the news of going home, a part of Royelle was concerned she didn't know what she was going home to. She couldn't even remember half the questions the doctors asked or why she was in the hospital, to begin with. Had it not been for the whiteboard she had to read every morning and throughout the day, reminding her of why she was in the hospital when it occurred and the condition she now faced, she'd be completely in the dark.

And every time she read the words, Dissociative Amnesia also known as Situational Amnesia, and how it applied to her, it broke her down. She hated that she had a brain functioning at what she considered to be its lowest potential. It made her feel incompetent despite being able to remember so many other important things and people in her life.

"Heyyyy, girl." Raylina happily said, walking into Royelle's room.

"Heyyy." Royelle smiled, excited to see them.

"How you feeling, big head?" Raymelle asked.

"I'm good. Just ready to go home."

"I know you are. The doctor been in here yet?" He asked.

"Yes. She's writing up the orders. She said, one of the nurses will be back to discharge me."

"Well, they need to come on with it. But let's get you dressed while they do that." Raylina said, excited to help her sister put on her clothes.

Seeing the same faces every day lit Royelle up. Xandra, with her early dawn visits, Raymelle and Raylina stayed consistent with their 9:30 slots, and Charlyn showed up as often as she could right before court just to check in, and today was no different. Royelle didn't care how short the visits were; it was the regularity that mattered. However, she couldn't ignore the lack of Rayford's presence, but she didn't want to bother her siblings about it. So she left it alone to discuss directly with him at another time.

The nurse entered the room with a wheelchair in tow, surprised to see Raymelle, Raylina, and Charlyn in the room. "Aren't you spoiled ?" The nurse joked. Royelle gave her a half-smile. She was ready to go and didn't care for the humor. Picking up on the dryness of the room, the nurse shifted from the pleasantries and got down to business. She handed Royelle the discharge summary, which included a list of the medications she could take for pain, headaches, and nausea. Additionally, it had Dr. Pisces and Dr.

Schwartz's office hours and phone numbers along with the name of Dr. Angeli, a Neuropsychologist that Dr. Pisces highly recommended.

"Do you have any questions for me, Royelle?" The nurse asked after her spiel.

"No, ma'am."

"Great. If I can get you to sign your name here and here, we can get you on your way."

Royelle grabbed the pen and scribbled her name on each line. She didn't care how sloppy the signature looked. She was ready to go. Once done, the nurse locked the wheels on the wheelchair while Raymelle helped Royelle into it. And although she didn't need it, it was hospital protocol.

"Do you have everything?" The nurse asked.

Royelle nodded yes. Once the nurse received confirmation, she began pushing Royelle to the elevators, and everyone followed until they exited the front lobby doors.

"Raylina. Take my truck and drive with Royelle to the house. I'm gonna ride with Charlyn, so she don't ride alone. We'll meet y'all there."

When the valet brought Raymelle's truck over, Raylina got in while he and Charlyn helped Royelle into the passenger side. As soon as Raylina pulled off, Charlyn and Raymelle went in the opposite direction, walking towards her car.

"Slow down, honey. Why are you walking so fast? Do you even know where you're going?" Charlyn laughed.

"My bad, Charlyn. I'm just all over the place. Now that she'll be home, how do I start to tell her about all the bullshit that's been going on?"

If it was a lot for him to handle, he couldn't imagine how his sister would take it; and that's even if she could. With the way her brain was operating, the shit that was concerning him and everyone else might not have the same effect on Royelle. But the only way to know was to give her the real. Charlyn suggested that they wait until they got to Royelle's to see where she was at mentally. He agreed.

For the next few minutes, the ride was silent. Unknown to the other, they were both in sync with their thoughts. They were equally trying to figure out how they would tell Royelle that Trevion was dead. But they also had to tell her that they didn't know where he was, if he was buried or cremated and that he was married to someone else. Not to mention, she probably had no rights to his assets, and to add salt to an open wound, Adala was gone. It was a lot for someone who didn't have a brain condition. But, for someone with Royelle's diagnosis, they just didn't know how she would handle it.

In all of Charlyn's years of practicing law, this was the worst case of lies, betrayal, and deceit she had ever seen. Even she was dumbfounded and without a clue as to what to do next. It was the first time Charlyn felt defeated in and out of the court. But like everyone surrounding Royelle, she would stop at nothing to get answers.

Raymelle continued to think about all the shit he knew and didn't know about Trevion. It fucked with him knowing that Trevion had played his entire family. But as a man, this was personal for him. He was created and raised to protect his family. So, welcoming Trevion into his family's world, trusting that he would do what he promised, only for it not to be followed through, burned him inside. And like Charlyn, nothing was going to stop him from getting to the grit of the dirt.

He began to Google every public profile website he could find and found it strange that the only thing that continued to come up was Trevion's construction company. In most cases on the search engines, you can find at least one or two things that relate to the person you're searching for. In this case, there was absolutely nothing related to Trevion's history, previous addresses, possible relatives, former employers, nothing.

Even his murder was mum. While it was odd, it wasn't uncommon. Unless the media made it to the scene of a crime, a lot of the murders went unreported, or they had a three-line article somewhere in the paper that most people overlooked. But Raymelle figured if Trevion lied about his life, then there was a chance he had also lied about his name, and what Raymelle was looking for on Trevion was really just a pin needle in a garbage dump landfill. It was going to take more than a Google search to get to the truth about Trevion.

"They got here fast," Charlyn said, looking at Raymelle's truck in the driveway.

"I mean, you were only going 20 miles an hour." Raymelle laughed, surprised to see Raylina still sitting in his truck with Royelle.

"Why y'all still out here?" Raymelle asked, walking towards them.

"Royelle won't get out of the truck." Raylina irritably answered.

"Whatchu mean? Why?"

"I don't know why. Ask her." Raylina opened the truck door and got out with an attitude.

When Xandra heard all the voices, she peeked out the window, glad to see her sister was finally home. But Raylina's visible irritation concerned her as she watched her move away from the truck, Raymelle get in, and Charlyn walk over to the passenger side. As she continued to look on, she didn't feel the need to intervene in a situation that was already being handled. Coupled with that was the contriteness she was still feeling. She felt uncomfortable giving any directives or speaking out of place. The pangs of guilt had her acting differently towards Royelle, and she hated it.

"Royelle, honey. Why don't we get you inside and get you situated?" Charlyn suggested.

Royelle said nothing and continued to sit in the truck with a blank look on her face as she stared at her house. It was as if she was trying to piece her life back together through the lens of a camera. And for the next twenty minutes, Raymelle and Charlyn tried to talk to Royelle and get a feel for what she was thinking or how she was feeling, but she wouldn't respond. She continued to be lost in thought as she stared at the house.

"Royelle. Listen to me—"

"Can we go inside, please?" Royelle cut Raymelle square off as if she was tired of waiting on him.

Charlyn opened the door, and Royelle slowly began to exit.

"Bout damn time," Raylina muttered under her breath.

"Yo, shut up." Raymelle mouthed back with an angry expression on his face.

Raylina thought she was safe by murmuring, but Raymelle's nosey ass could hear the whispers of voices from two blocks away and read the most lulled of lips. Once inside the house, everyone stopped what they were doing and let Royelle dictate their next move. She stopped in front of the stairs and stared at them as if climbing them would be the longest climb of her life. No one knew what to make of her tenor or what she was thinking, but they knew she was trying to make sense of something. They assumed her mind must've been soullessly empty, or it was trying to put the pieces of her life back together.

"Raylina, go start a bath for her." Raymelle directed.

She looked over at him with an irritated look. But, when she saw his lips mouth the words, *"go get some sleep medicine,"* it was then that she realized what he was about to do. She quickly went upstairs, turned the water on to a hot, comfortable level, and added some Rice Sake bubble bath to it. Had Royelle been with the times, she would've choked the hell out of Raylina for opening her $82.00 bottle of bubble bath that she was savoring for the right time and occasion. But, it was either that or the Prosecco bubble bath that Raylina knew Royelle only used when she sipped on her Prosecco Wine out of a tulip glass. And since it wasn't that kind of party, and there were no other options, Rice Sake Bath it was. She grabbed the sleeping pills out of the medicine cabinet as she was told, stuck them in her pocket, and headed back downstairs.

"All set, brother," Raylina said, walking down the stairs.

"A'ight sis. You heard Ray. Ready when you are."

Without provocation, Royelle began marching up the stairs at a plodding pace one step at a time. "Home Sweet Home." Royelle softly said as Charlyn followed closely behind her. Raylina handed Raymelle the pills and went back up the stairs to be with her sister.

"Fool! Are you getting ready to do what I think you're gonna do?" Xandra asked as they walked into the kitchen.

"Hell yea! Do you wanna stay up with her all night trying to explain to her how fucked up her life is right now?"

"Shit! Is it gonna matter? Cause we gotta tell her one of these days. Especially about Momma."

"You right, sis. But it won't be tonight. Her ass is going to sleep."

Xandra laughed as she watched Raymelle grab the *crack* Iced tea as they called it out of the fridge. He crushed up the sleeping pills and dropped them in her drink before warming it up. Since he and Raylina made the tea as sweet as Royelle liked it, Raymelle knew it would be hard for her to detect the taste of anything else. Before going upstairs, he grabbed a piece of mail from the mail organizer that hung on the wall and wrote a note on the back of the envelope.

"You coming?" Raymelle asked as he proceeded to leave the kitchen with the glass of tea.

"Nah. Imma stay here. If I go up there, she ain't never gonna sleep." Xandra replied.

By the time he made it upstairs, he was surprised to see Royelle already lying down naked with a sheet and quilt covering her.

"Damn, that was quick, sis! You sure you wiped your ass, right?" He joked.

"She wanted to take a quick shower, so we didn't force the bubble bath issue," Charlyn replied.

"Nah, that's cool. As long as she's comfortable, that's all that matters. Here. Drink this crack. It's just the way you like it; lukewarm and full of diabetes." He chuckled.

Royelle was bland. No smile, no laughter, no nothing. She reached out for the glass, gulped it down, and handed the glass right back to him. She turned over and pulled the comforter up to her ears. She was done for the night, which was fine by him. He was just glad that she drank it all. The goal was to put her out for the night, hoping that she would be of sound mind to receive what was coming in the morning. He walked over to what used to be Trevion's side of the bed and left the note he wrote on the envelope right in front of their wedding picture.

CHAPTER 19:
SHATTERED

*R*oyelle woke up the next day, and the first thing she saw looking back at her was her huge modern 3D wall clock with mirror numbers, letting her know it was 9:43 in the morning. She was shocked to see that she had slept through the morning, something she never did. She quickly tried to get up, but a crushing, throbbing, pounding pain sent jolts of agony to the front and back of her skull. It made her feel like she was carrying a pallet of cinder blocks on her head.

She slowly laid back down and closed her eyes in the hopes that it might help to wait a moment, but the aches wouldn't let up. It was as if the pain didn't allow room for her to feel or sense anything outside of the torture it was dosing her. She laid still for another twenty minutes with her eyes closed and relaxed her mind. Once she felt a sense of calm come over her, rather than to raise her head, this time she rolled herself over to the edge of the bed and slowly sat up.

While her head was still hurting, it was manageable now. '*I must've sat up too quickly last time,*' she said to herself, convinced that it couldn't have been anything else. None of what happened in the last twenty-four hours, days, or weeks seemed to have affected her in any way. She slowly stood up and paced herself as she walked over to the windows she liked to pray in front of. She opened her curtains and took a deep breath as she inhaled the rays from the sun and exhaled the warmth it produced. She loved the sun, it was her reminder that all days were blessed days.

As she got ready to bend down for her daily prayer, the thought of kneeling with the headache she was experiencing was too much. But she knew God, and knew that He didn't care if she was standing, kneeling, sitting, or squatting on the toilet; as long as she was speaking to him, it was pleasing. She turned and sat down in the same recliner that Trevion sat on during the many nights he pleasured himself as he watched other men have their way with her. But when she closed her eyes, it wasn't the peace of God that met her. She was succumbed by vague flashes of EMT's hovering over a female, yelling and prepping her while she lay on the gurney.

She was so disturbed by the oddities she couldn't even begin her prayer, let alone finish it. She quickly opened her eyes and struggled to slow down her heavy breathing. She tried to make sense of the vision she saw, but nothing came of it. In a panic, unbalanced on her feet and all, she made her way back to the bed, but the sudden movement caused her head to spin again. "Urgh," she said, grabbing her head in an attempt to slow down the spin cycle motion.

Once she sat down and was able to get her mind and body at a steady pace, she slowly began to assess everything in the room until her eyes finally honed in on the wedding photo of her and Trevion sitting on top of the nightstand that was on his side of the bed. She quickly looked down at her left hand, shocked to see a huge diamond on her ring finger, and wondered how she managed to overlook it when she first woke up.

She furrowed her eyebrows as she walked to the opposite side of her California King size bed. When she reached the nightstand, she picked up the picture and the note Raymelle left for her. *'Sis, today is a new day for you. Things might be weird right now. But when you're ready to talk, come downstairs.'* If confusion was a person, Royelle was it. She stared at the picture and the note for several minutes and couldn't make heads or tails regarding any of it.

But, she was more concerned about the wedding picture than she was anything else. She was stumped at the fact that there she was looking like a

Royal Queen, standing in front of a man who she assumed was supposed to be her Royal King, on what she presumed was their Royal wedding day, but she had no remembrance of him or that day.

She stared at the picture some more, hoping that looking at it might help her remember him, that day, those clothes, his smile, the scenery, something, anything, but nothing happened. She put the picture down, slowly walked into the closet, and noticed that the only clothes there belonged to her. She walked back out, looked at the picture again, and began looking inside the nine dresser drawers, only to find nothing.

'What is going on? Am I being punked?' She thought to herself, looking back at the picture.

She lagged over to the Espresso chest, checked those drawers, went into the bathroom, looked under the sink, scanned the medicine cabinet, and to her surprise, not a single thing related to the male species was found. Now she had questions. She picked up the picture along with the note and headed out of the room, looking for Raymelle.

Quietly, she stepped out and heard voices coming from the kitchen area. She panicked when she picked up on Charlyn's. *'I'm about to be in serious trouble.'* She said to herself. The last thing she needed was to be chastised by her boss. Right now, her focus was to find out who the man in the photo was.

"Good Morning." She said, stepping into the kitchen.

Charlyn, Raymelle, and Xandra all jumped at the sound of her voice. Neither of them was expecting her to be out of the bed, let alone clutching her wedding picture in her right hand. She casually placed the picture down on the table, walked over towards her Cranberry Red K-Elite Keurig, and began to prepare herself a cup of her favorite Folgers Caramel Drizzle coffee.

They each watched as she carefully took all the necessary steps to make her K-Cup. They were expecting a different her, but she appeared to act as if nothing was wrong, as if it was just like a typical day for her. But, because they knew things were new in her world, they, too, had to move differently. The same level of joking and bullshitting they did with her in the past, they could do no more. The Royelle they remember was a bit different, and it showed. Dealing with this new Royelle was going to be a challenge that no one was equipped for, at least not yet.

"Charlyn, I'm really sorry about today. I don't know how or why I overslept like that. I almost pulled a no-call, no-show." Royelle said as she continued to fix her coffee.

"Correction, young lady. You did pull a no call, no show." Charlyn laughed.

"Well, yes, I stand corrected." Royelle turned towards Charlyn, giggling. "Howeverrr, you know it's unlike me to not show up for work or call if I was running late. Which is why you're here, right? To find out why I didn't make it to work? I mean, why else would two of the very people who never come to my house be here now and uninvited, might I add."

"Uninvited?! You got me fucked up! I don't need no damn invite." Raymelle laughed.

"Neither do I." Charlyn followed.

"And I'm always here. So, I don't count." Xandra chimed in

"Oh, stop it, guys. You all know what I mean." Royelle said as she took her seat.

She held her forehead in the palm of her left hand, calmly pouring the creamer into her favorite mug with her right. The mug read, *Good Morning, THIS IS GOD. I will be handling ALL YOUR PROBLEMS today*. It was the right kind of mug for the moments she had experienced and the ones she was about to face. Raymelle taking note of her weary yet alert mannerisms, wasn't sure if he should seize the moment or leave it alone. But, they had to start somewhere and hoped that Royelle would be receptive to everything they had to share with her.

"Sis, you a'ight?" Raymelle asked.

"Honestly, I feel like I was run over by a train. My head is killing me."

She lifted her head slightly enough to catch a glimpse of the wedding photo she forgot she had put on the table. With razor-sharp eyes, she turned her complete attention to the picture and grabbed it as the others looked on. The room was silent. Instead of speaking, they watched as if they were afraid to do or say anything out of fear that they could set her back or cause her to do something crazy.

"You wanna talk about it, sis?" Raymelle asked, noticing her questioning disposition.

"Talk? Talk about what?"

"First about your ugly ass face." He joked, trying to ease any rising tensions.

Royelle didn't bite. She continued to stare at the picture, not the least bit concerned with Raymelle's tomfoolery. She was too busy in her own head trying to make sense of what she was looking at. Noticing her disregard towards him, he knew joking wasn't the way to go. So, without further delay, he said what needed to be said.

"Sis, do you remember being in a car accident?"

"Car accident? " She scowled.

Neither of the three knew the right way to explain it. They weren't professionals in the Psychology of the mind. So, someone would have to explain it the best way they knew how. But before they could start to speak, Royelle began again.

"I don't remember the accident. I remember the doctors telling me about the accident."

"Well, that's good," Raymelle said with a sigh of relief.

"Can y'all tell me more about it?"

Everyone was excited that, for the moment, she was good. She was open and willing to talk, and that was the first step. So, rather than spend countless hours explaining the details, Charlyn opened up the photo gallery on her phone that showed the pictures Trooper Wright took for her. "Swipe to the right," Charlyn said, passing the phone to Royelle.

They all looked on as Royelle looked at the pictures in shock. She couldn't believe she was looking at pictures of her car and what looked like her near-death experience. She knew that the accident was one from which only God and the angels he had on assignment could have saved her. She couldn't believe her eyes. Since the pictures were time and date stamped, there was no question about when the accident happened; the question now was how it happened and why?

She looked back at the 8x10 and asked. "Who is this? And is he the reason for all of this?" She pointed down at the crash scene photos.

Raymelle sighed. "Sis, this is Trevion. Your husband." He responded.

"Husband! I-I-I don't have a husband!" She stuttered. "Y'all need to stop playing with me for real. What kind of sick game is this? Trust me; I would remember having a husband." She retorted.

Given the perplexed look on her face, they could tell she was very agitated and confused, not realizing that she still had no idea about how much her life had changed in the weeks she laid dormant in her hospital bed. And since she seemed to be driven by photo evidence, Raymelle pulled out his phone and opened up Royelle's Facebook page and photo albums going back five years, hoping that this would give her a complete picture of her life with Trevion.

"Here. Look at this." He passed her the phone.

When she looked at the timeline, it supplied her with a sequence of events. Starting from when they first got together, got married, honeymooned, brought their house, the time he supported her through her mother's diagnoses, and when he surprised her with Chasity, just to name a few. They watched as she puzzlingly scrolled and scrolled through the pictures, each of them wishing they could read her thoughts. They wanted to say something but didn't want to add to the already mounting pressure they could tell was building inside of her.

"I know it's not making any sense to you right now, but…"

"Stop!" She put her right palm up, cutting Raymelle off.

With her face screwed up, she tightly closed her eyes while she took a moment to think; to process; to readjust. She inhaled deeply and opened her eyes while exhaling.

"Ok. Start over, Raymelle. Who is this? And why don't I remember him?"

Raymelle and Xandra both looked over at Charlyn, who, in their opinion, was the best person to answer those questions for Royelle. It seemed right and made the most sense since she was there from the beginning to the end. Bit by bit, Charlyn began giving Royelle all the details of what led to her accident while Raymelle and Xandra looked on and stayed quiet. And the more Charlyn spoke, the more Royelle cried. She couldn't believe the reality she was being faced with. *Murder? Married? To two women? Amnesia? How?* She thought. She was in complete disbelief as her mind scrambled for any sense of rationality. What she was hearing just couldn't be. None of it made sense. Her life was always perfect as far as she could tell and remember. This, what she was hearing, didn't happen to good people like her. She was confounded.

She couldn't understand how she could remember everything about the people sitting in front of her but couldn't remember a man she was supposedly married to and had been with for five years. How could a person not remember someone like that? Someone you share your every thought with, your sheets, your time, your good, and your bad. It was unfathomable for her to grasp. It wasn't just that he was murdered, or that she was married to him and couldn't remember him, but it was also learning that he was married to someone else before her. Hearing that led her to question herself as a solid woman. She couldn't believe that she would get involved with a married man and then marry him. Wasn't that illegal? Who would allow such a thing? And what kind of woman did that make her? Her mother raised her better than that she thought, as the tears streamed down. There was just no way that the life she couldn't remember was the life she was actually living.

"Sis, say something," Raymelle said after five minutes of silence.

"Let me get this straight. I've been in a horrible car accident and ended up in a coma after learning that the man I'm married to has been murdered and has another wife, all of which caused me to get this diss-ah whatever it's called amnesia. Because of said amnesia, I have blocked him and anything related to him out of my memory. Does that about sum it up?" She cut her eyes over at Raymelle. Before he could answer, she jumped back in.

"Did the doctor at least say how long I will be like this? Because it seems that this Trevion character left a huge mess behind for me to clean up in the wake of his demise. Or do I clean it up at all? Is that his real wife's job? I'm so confused about what is happening in my life right now." She angered.

"I understand, Royelle. And we're going to take care of this one step and day at a time. But your healing comes first. As for the doctor, no, she didn't say. She said over time, with you seeing all the right specialists, they'll be able to help you regain that part of the memory that you've disassociated yourself from." Charlyn said.

"Ha! Now that's a word. Disassociated! Seems like something I would do with or without memory loss had I known about his true self before. I am Royelle Blevins. The daughter of the most beautiful, moral, god-fearing woman I know. I was raised not to get involved with the likes of someone like this piece of shit. Disassociated?! Absolutely!" She rolled her neck. "So, given all this information and what Charlyn just said, what would you like for me to say, Raymelle? Hmm? What exactly?" She bantered. "Sounds to me like not only does my life have an entire period missing from it, but it also feels like it's in complete and utter fucking shambles. So, tell me, Raymelle. What would you say? How would you fucking feel if you were in my shoes?" She crossed her arms and looked up at him with a blank stare.

They were all stumped. In fact, they were very surprised at her brashness and tone. That had never been her character. So to see it now was a bit startling but understandable at the same time. They knew there would be some changes with her and thought they'd be ready when they came; they thought wrong. Since she didn't get the answer she was looking for, she looked back down at the phone to scroll some more and quickly looked back up just in time to catch the three of them weirdly looking at each other.

"So, what's up? I see the way that you all are staring at each other. There's more, isn't there? What else did I miss during my time of slumber, Raymelle?" She angrily asked. "And don't lie to me!" She slammed the phone on the table.

His hesitation in answering her question only infuriated her more.

"You minus well tell me whatever it is now, Raymelle. Let's just get it out in the open. After all, I do have amnesia, right? So, who's to say I'm going to remember it anyway. Just spit it!" The way she spoke so impudently made everyone uncomfortable. The way she was behaving wasn't her, and the slight changes they were starting to see were unsettling. "Well! Spill it!" She yelled.

"Man, chill the fuck out. That's enough!" Raymelle snapped.

"I am chill! But your energy is weird, so I know there's more. Just say what needs to be said, Raymelle."

The truth was, Raymelle didn't want to get any deeper into the conversation than they already were. He didn't want to keep poking the untamed bear that had become his sister. But since she knew her brother wasn't good with emotions, the look on his face told her everything she needed to know without it being said.

"It's Momma, isn't it?" She bluntly asked.

The delay in his response was her confirmation.

"When Ray?" She cried.

He hesitated to answer.

"Ray! When?!" She hollered.

"A few weeks after you went into the coma." He sulked.

She didn't ask about Rayford's attendance during Adala's transition, nor did she care to know. The less she knew about his involvement in any of it, the better. Besides, Raymelle wasn't ready to give her the scoop on the bullshit Rayford had done since she was in the hospital. He wanted to save that for another day. She was already dealing with enough.

"Did you honor all her wishes, Ray?"

"To the nine's." He responded. "I'm sorry that shit happened like this, sis."

"Sorry? Sorry for what? This is God's timing. We can't do anything about that. I'm sorry I wasn't there."

She inhaled and instantly felt tremendous pressure building up inside her as her breathing began to stutter into her lungs. She tried to control the flow of tears, but they gushed like a wild river. For several minutes the only sounds heard were the painful wailings of Royelle's cries. They knew the level of pain she would face once she processed that her mother was no longer with them. Raymelle scrolled through his phone to the picture that Raylina sent him of their mother and gave it to Royelle.

"Oh, my goddd!" She weeped.

She couldn't believe how beautiful her mother looked lying there in such peace. She continued to look at the picture and ball. Her cries were so painful that they caused the others to shed tears; even unsympathetic ass Xandra was letting go for once. But as soon as she accepted her mother's fate and how tranquil she looked, her breathing returned to normal, and it was back to business. Her body language, attitude, and demeanor quickly changed. The mourning she was displaying for her mother almost appeared fake the way she switched up. No tears, no cracking in her voice, just straight talk as if nothing had happened a few minutes prior. She was faced with so much that she didn't know what to deal with first or how to manage her emotions behind it.

"I'm shattered y'all. This is a lot to take in, and I honestly don't know what to say or how to feel at this very moment."

"You're entitled to feel however you want to feel at this point. Your feelings are valid, Royelle." Charlyn reminded.

While it was great that she could remember everything concerning her work, family, daily routines, personal business affairs, and such, not associating her life and emotions to someone she was married to made her feel incomplete. She felt like she woke up half a woman, half sane, half alive, half available to the world. She didn't say another word. She finished her coffee, excused herself from the table, and headed upstairs to take a much-needed shower. When Royelle left, Charlyn opened her briefcase, took out three packs of Sticky Post-It notes, and placed them on the table.

"What are we supposed to do with these?" Xandra asked.

"Since there are five stacks of pads in each pack, that should give us plenty to write down anything we can remember that will help her with her memory. Since she can't remember anything connected to Trevion, between the three of us, we need to write down everything about him and their marriage and place the notes everywhere, starting with the rooms upstairs and then his office."

No one objected to the idea. And since Royelle wasn't in therapy yet, this was a way to try and help her retain some of her loss. Or, at minimum, it would benefit them from having to repeat what she couldn't remember about him or the accident. Once they understood what Charlyn was trying to do, they all started writing.

By the time they reached upstairs, they had found Royelle sleeping under Raylina in the guest room. They quietly entered the room and placed notes all over the mirrors and the backside of the guest door. They took the same approach with her bedroom and the master bath. The idea was to leave no stone unturned. They were all adamant about Royelle getting back to herself as soon as possible, and this was the best way to start.

CHAPTER 20:
THE BEGINNING OF THE END

*R*oyelle handled the death of her mother better than anyone would've expected. They all knew how close she was to Adala and how devasted she would be behind her passing, but to their surprise, she didn't speak much about it and carried on like normal. Unbeknownst to them, she was deeply hurt by Adala's passing, but was prepared for it long before it happened. The plans that Raymelle and Rayford were shocked about at the funeral home, Royelle was already a part of from the first day her mother decided on it.

Once the decision was made, Royelle purchased herself and Raylina Rose Gold Cremation Urn necklaces. It was embellished with their mother's Light Amethyst birthstone, a half of an Angel Wing, and a see-through Timecapulse Hourglass. Inscribed on it were the words, *"I will forever remember my name."* It was gorgeous. And for Raymelle, since he was a man's man, she got him a Stainless Steel Bullet Urn necklace that had a cross in the middle of it with the Lord's Prayer circling around it and had them all mailed directly to Joann.

When it was time for Raymelle to pick up the remains, Joann had all the necklaces, and traditional urn for Rayford blessed with Adala's ashes. He was shocked but not surprised to see what his sister had done. She was very much like their mother when it came down to preparation, and it showed. The moment Royelle put the necklace around her neck, was the moment she vowed to wear strength. It was one of the many things her mother taught her to always have. Therefore, she wore it proudly, knowing that her mother would always be with her, reminding her of her steps.

While she was locked and loaded in preparation for Adala, nothing could have prepared for the accident, coma, and the news about Trevion or another wife. She was mind warped since they told her about it all. And although her memory surrounding Trevion was shit, her family made it their business to make sure she wouldn't forget for long. Each time she opened her eyes and moved about the house, it was his picture and sticky notes about him that she saw and read.

And from the very first day she woke up surrounded by the notes, she knew she was going to have to be an investigator of her own kind. It was just a matter of getting started. To get the answers she needed, she created a timeline of her thoughts, emotions, and ideas in what she called her brain diary journal.

Based on what she learned from her family and Charlyn, she listed everything about Trevion in chronological order and studied it like a bible. It was her way of training her brain to remember. It wasn't the easiest of processes for her, and she didn't know if her method was working, but the thought of it was good enough for her.

Day in and day out, folks who knew about Royelle's situation, those who worked with Trevion, and people who claimed to be his friend came to see her often to offer their support and condolences; and she hated it. Unfortunately, no amount of love, support, back rubs, and talks about how everything was going to be ok would help with the level of hurt and confusion she was experiencing.

Despite the house being full of people everyday, she still felt like she was the only person standing in it. She felt like people were acting weird and often looked around at them, wondering how many of them really knew the truth about Trevion? Did any of them really care for how she felt? Were they really there to offer support or just to be nosey? At this point, everyone she looked at was the usual suspect. She wasn't sure how to feel about any of them or what to believe in their actions or words. She didn't know who she could trust with her emotions or the little that was left of her heart. Therefore, she trusted absolutely no one outside of her siblings. She couldn't see past the red tape.

It wasn't that people were acting funny, they just didn't know what to say or how to perceive her standoff-ish demeanor. Everyone who came to see and support her understood that she was in a shattered place; she just didn't realize how deeply fragmented she was. Some days she came out of her room and sat amongst the guest as they quietly mingled with each other, trying not to make her feel uncomfortable. Other days, she didn't so much as get out of bed to take a bath or brush her teeth. It mattered none. People were still coming in droves to show their love and respect.

"Knock Knock," Raymelle said before walking into Royelle's room.

She didn't move a muscle. She stayed lying in the same fetal position she was in when he last checked on her.

"Say lil mama. You plan on getting up sometime today?" He joked, hoping to get a smile.

Royelle stayed silent.

"Look, sis." Raymelle walked over towards the bed. "I know this shit is complicated, but no one can make any moves until you do. So, tell me what else we can do to help you through this."

Royelle said nothing and continued to stare at the wedding picture, unable to control her tears.

"It's gonna be a'ight sis." He said in a concerned tone.

With sad, sunken eyes, Royelle scooted back on the bed slightly as Raymelle sat down.

"I'm good, bro." She said, wiping her tears. " I just get in my moments where I look at all these pictures, read all these notes, and it tells me that there was a time when I believed and trusted in that man. But the truth is, I never really knew him and now look at this mess. Here's this dead man, who is supposed to be married to someone other than me. I don't remember anything about him, and I don't know if he's been buried or cremated. I can't even get access to his medical records to do some research, and I don't know who his family is cause I don't know who he is. Do you see where I am going with this Melle?" She asked with a dejected look.

"Sis. You have every right to be confused and upset about it. No one is taking that from you. And trust me, you might not remember everything now, but you're strong and smart as shit! You said it yourself. You're Adala Blevins, daughter! And because of that, everything is gonna come back to you, watch! I ain't got no doubt about it. And when it does, I'll be right here for whatever you need. You hear me?" He said in an unfeigned tone.

They locked eyes with an understanding that it's already done. Raymelle took a deep breath, kissed his sister on her forehead, and let her know he'd be right downstairs if she needed anything.

As she watched her brother walk out of the room, she couldn't help but to think that he might have felt just as bamboozled as she had. Since she saw the proof that they had been together for five years, it was fair to say that she wasn't the only one affected by the treachery and deception that beset Trevion. Everyone connected to her was, and that was a violation.

She laid down for a few more minutes and decided that once she got out of that bed, she wouldn't lie down idle again until she found out everything there was to know and learn about Trevion. She knew it wasn't gonna be easy, but she was willing to try and do anything to help with her mental instability surrounding him. And more than that, she was on a hunt to get as much information about his supposed other wife.

"Ok, Royelle Blevins," she said as she sat up, swinging her feet over to the side of the bed. "You can do this. You have beat better odds than this. You can do this." She repeated while grasping her mother's urn.

Even though her memory was a bit shotty, there was no purer vision when it came down to remembering that only God could see her through this. She walked over to her usual praying spot and kneeled. The way her legs and knees ached as they simultaneously worked together was a stark reminder that it had been a while since she had prayed in a kneeling position. But, before she could begin praying, a barrage of thoughts and emotions came over her again. But this time, it caused her to turn her anger towards God. It was as if Satan intercepted the play while she was standing in the end zone. Her whole demeanor had changed in an instant.

She got up from the floor and walked back over to where the picture sat atop the nightstand. She picked up the frame, screamed, and with all the strength she could muster up, she punched the frame causing all the glass to break. There were so many people downstairs talking and carrying on that no one heard a thing. She ripped the picture out, flung the frame across the other side of the room, and began tearing the picture into tiny little pieces.

"For whatever you've done! For whoever you really are! And for everything you have done to me, lied to me about, or put me through, you will rot in hell for all of it! You mark my words, you son of a bitch! You're a piece of shit and a waste of space! How could any real woman want your trifling ass?! Especially me!" She yelled.

Royelle continued to tear the picture up into as many pieces as she could make, disregarding the blood running down her hand from the cut caused by the glass. Once she was done ripping it apart, she hurled the shreds into the air and watched as they landed in scattered places throughout the bedroom floor, with half of Trevion's face landing at her feet.

"Urghhh! Fuck you! Even in death, you're trying to torture me!"

She bent down, picked up the half picture, tore it up some more, and discarded it into the small wastebasket beside her nightstand, all to avoid seeing his face any further. She was all out of love, understanding, and patience. She sat back down on the bed, eyeballing the mess she made between the broken glass and the picture, when she noticed the droplets of blood on the floor. "Shit!" She said, looking down at her hand. She walked into the bathroom, turned the water to lukewarm temperature, and let it run over her hand.

Continuing to stare at the mess, she thought about the police, the hospitals, and everyone she, Charlyn, Raymelle, and Xandra had tried to contact regarding Trevion's whereabouts. They all wanted Royelle and her people to believe that Royelle's hands were tied and she should leave well enough alone. But that wasn't good enough for Royelle. It was that very thinking from others that kick-started her incineration fuel.

Any Christian-like reasonings God may have made with her in the past, at this point, were gone. Before, all she had to do was think about something her mother said or a scripture she read out of the bible. Now, no matter how powerful or influential those words were in the past, they were now a blur for Royelle. It was a no-brainer that the devil was the driving force behind Royelle's current spin, and it was just getting started. Seemingly, a different Royelle, whether she knew it, cared to admit it, recognized, or acknowledged it, was being born. Hell hath no fury as a woman scorned, and the devil was ready to dance.

Once she noticed the blood was no longer an issue, she dried her hands and covered the small cut with a band-aid. Royelle's mind was on 100! She had so many things running through it. She opened up her brain diary to see if there were any clues that she could follow, and to her surprise, she found one of her recent entries.

'Royelle, you've tried everything you could to get more answers about Trevion. Nothing has come to pass. Try setting up a memorial service. It will bring people in from everywhere. Find a function hall to host it at, announce it in every newspaper you can think of, post it on social media and let the investigation begin. Make sure to tell Xandra so she knows what to do. She can and will help you with this. Whatever you don't remember, Xandra will remember for you. A memorial service is a great place to start. It's the beginning of the end.'

CHAPTER 21:
IT'S YOU AGAIN

*T*he moment Amadeo told AJ about Royelle's accident, her life had slightly shifted. It perturbed her that she had no way of checking on Royelle daily, and she had no access to her at the hospital. When she called the hospital to get information, they asked for an access code that she didn't have. And when AJ tried to see her, AJ's name wasn't on the list of approved visitors. Since she couldn't get a hold of Xandra and didn't have anyone else's number to call, she set her energy on praying for Royelle to wake up and get better.

When Xandra finally reached out and let AJ know that Royelle was home, although excited, she battled with the decision on whether to call Royelle or not. AJ was afraid of rejection and wasn't mentally prepared for an absent-minded Royelle. The dread of Royelle not remembering her or their secret kept her from reaching out to Royelle like she normally would have under different circumstances.

She stood by her bedroom window, staring at the sky, trying to build up the courage to call Royelle and deal with whatever was coming her way. It had been long enough, and she had to see her. Besides, the way Amadeo had the house somber-ridden since Trevion's death drove AJ nuts. She needed to get out. And despite what was happening with Royelle, she was the peace that AJ sought after. Therefore, she hit the first number on her list of favorites, and the phone instantly dialed out Royelle's number. When the phone began ringing, AJ grew increasingly nervous, not knowing what version of Royelle she would get, but she was ready.

"Hello," Royelle answered.

AJ Froze at the sound of Royelle's sweet voice. She wasn't expecting her to answer so quickly. "Hey Royelle, it's AJ." She quickly identified herself.

"Good Morning AJ. I know who you are. Caller ID." Royelle giggled.

"I'm sorry, Royelle. I just —"

"I know." Royelle cut in. "You just wanted to make sure I'd remember you. Everybody does it. Don't worry. I remember a lot despite what people might think." Royelle laughed.

Xandra had warned AJ about Royelle's mental disconnection from anything that was associated with Trevion. Therefore, the fact that Royelle remembered her quickly put her at ease. After all, Trevion was the reason she and Royelle even knew each other to begin with. The last thing AJ wanted was for the flame between her and Royelle to go out because of her connection to Trevion. But, what AJ didn't know was that, Royelle's brain registered something special between them. Therefore, her memory never coupled AJ with the likes of Trevion.

"How are you, AJ?" Royelle asked.

"Me? I'm fine. The question is, how are you?"

"I am as good as can be expected, I guess. Why haven't I seen or heard from you?"

AJ paused. She was feeling twice as bad now. She wanted to call Royelle on many occasions, but out of fear, always decided against it.

"To be completely honest, I was petrified that you wouldn't remember me, and I wasn't ready to handle that."

"Seee, that's what's you get for assuming. So when will I get to see you again?"

"As long as you're asking, whenever you're ready." AJ smiled.

"AJ, I'm home with no place to go, no time soon. You're welcome here anytime."

Royelle needed to say nothing more. They agreed to a visit and disconnected the call. AJ was so damn excited. She couldn't wait to get the hell out of the house and be around someone that brought joy no matter what they were going through. And the fact that Royelle remembered her made this moment all the more alluring.

Amadeo was sitting in the guest room with the television on ESPN and the volume low as he scrolled through his phone, looking at all the old text messages, pictures, and porn sites that he and Trevion shared. Even after thirty-plus days, he still couldn't believe that Trevion was gone. It was one unsettling thing that Trevion was dead; it was another to still be unclear as to who knew about their affair. It was unhinging for him to think that he might have to deal with that level of exposure by himself one day.

Seeing Amadeo grieve the way he had, made AJ feel bad for how she had previously acted towards him, regrading Trevion, especially now, seeing how badly Trevion's death was affecting him. While she didn't understand the reasoning behind the hard grief, she respected it. A lot was riding on his death.

While business deals and plans shouldn't have been the thing on people's minds, it was difficult not to think about them. His employees depended on the work, and the projects that Trevion had contracts with were in limbo. Not to mention, Amadeo and Trevion worked on projects that were sure to bring in some big bucks for him and Ajah. But now, thirty-some-odd days after Trevion's death, things were still uncertain. The only reason a few were still up and running was because of Amadeo's involvement in the board and business meetings.

And to make matters even more clouded, those who heard Trevion was supposedly married to someone else wondered if it was true. They wanted to know who she was, what she knew about the business, and if she would soon be in charge of the business undertakings that affected the way money flowed. The only person they knew and trusted to do any business plans and agreements with was Royelle, and she was in no position to do so at the moment.

By the time AJ walked into the guest room, Amadeo had locked his phone and was lying down, staring at the T.V., not paying any attention to its content. She stood in the doorway wondering if he was going to speak. But, he never looked her way as she waited on a hello, hi, what's up, what are you doing, something, anything. It was just dead air and space between them. Until she finally spoke.

"Hey, Deo. "How are you feeling today?" She asked.

"I'm good." He continued looking at the T.V.

"Are you sure you're ok?"

"What's up, Ajah? Did you need something," He dryly and rudely responded.

"You know what. No. I don't need anything," She snapped back. "I was just checking on you and wanted to let you know I'm going to Royelle's for a while. I'll be back later."

"Royelle's?!" Amadeo quickly sat up. "When are you going?"

"Ohhh, he speaks!" She sassed. "I'm leaving in the next hour or so."

"Good. I'm going with you."

AJ's eyes squinted, and her eyebrows frowned. "You wanna go with me?" She asked in a confused tone.

"Yea, why? Is that a problem for you?"

"No, Amadeo. And calm down. Don't make it a problem. I was just asking because I know you. When you're ready to go, you're ready to go, and I don't know how long I'm going to be over there."

"All right. Well, I'll follow you there. It's not a big deal."

Without another word, AJ turned around and walked back towards the master bedroom while Amadeo walked into the guest bathroom and started the shower. *'The hell is wrong with him.'* She thought as she walked away. He was quiet, and his attitude was rough. It was as if he was mad at AJ for Trevion's demise. Rather than embracing her at a time like this, he treated her like shit driving her further apart from him. She couldn't understand what all the hostility was about and figured if he was still mad at her for questioning him about Trevion, then the accusations must've had some truth to it. And as much as AJ wanted to find out what was going with him, she decided to let him be in his feelings until he was ready to talk.

Once she was done showering and getting dressed, she walked back into the guest room and saw Amadeo was showered, dressed, and waiting on her. Without another utter, she turned and walked towards the front door; Amadeo followed. They silently walked out of the house and to their cars. Shortly after leaving their house, they arrived at Royelle's, and like clockwork, since Royelle's return, the house was filled with people. The street was full of cars. There was nowhere to park in the driveway or on the street near her house.

AJ and Amadeo circled the block in the hopes of finding a good spot, but there was nothing. The only spots left were right in front of Mrs. Benton's house. The one place that it seemed everyone and their mother were avoiding to park in front of.

"Ain't this some shit! I don't wanna park here." AJ said as she paralleled parked her car into the tight spot. It gave her an eerie feeling knowing that she was parked dead smack in front of the house where a heinous murder had occurred not too long before Trevion's. It didn't feel right. Although AJ knew she wasn't disrespecting the dead by parking there, she still felt like she was.

Once she was done parking, she grabbed her belongings, stepped out of the car, and avoided as much eye contact with Mrs. Benton's house as possible. She began slowly walking away, forcing Amadeo to jog a little and catch up to her. As soon as he did, he grabbed her right hand and intertwined it with his left. She looked down, surprised at his public display of affection. It was the first time since Trevion's passing that he made any physical contact with her.

She gathered it was all for show. He must've wanted to prove to folks that the two were a united front, supportive, and totally in love with one another. But it was all fake, and she couldn't paint that picture for him or anybody else, no matter what the canvas depicted. As soon as they reached the door, she released his hand and read the note informing guests to let themselves inside. She slowly opened the door and immediately heard the multitude of voices throughout the house but wasn't interested in any of them. She was looking for Royelle and Royelle only.

"Hey! How y'all doing?" Raymelle asked, approaching Amadeo with an extended hand.

"Heyy, brother!" Amadeo responded, smiling.

"Thanks for coming." Raymelle hugged AJ.

"Thanks, not needed, Raymelle. How are you? How's Royelle doing?" AJ responded.

"She's hanging in there. She's upstairs with Xandra. You know that's like her German Shepard and Pitbull combined, always on guard protecting the package. Royelle can't even take a shit unless Xandra knows about it."

They all laughed.

"I can imagine! But that's what sisters do. They protect each other. Especially in times like these." AJ responded.

"You right! But make yourself at home, Ajah. They'll be down in a minute. Amadeo, something to drink?" Raymelle asked.

Raymelle had no idea how much at home she already felt. As he and Amadeo made their way to the kitchen to enjoy the smooth taste of the 1942 Tequila, the vivid memories of her and Royelle played out in her head. A slight smile graced her facial expressions as she looked around at all the people chilling and carrying about, on the very places she and Royelle had sex.

Like an animal, those were her marked territories, and seeing others around them, only made her want Royelle more, so she could remark the old ones and create new ones. It was the weirdest thing, but it was AJ's way of feeling solidified in Royelle's life. And now, with Trevion out of the picture, it would just be a matter of time.

AJ stood out of the way against the base of the stairs as she looked around at everyone that was in the house. And although she remembered a few faces from visiting the different sites, there wasn't anyone she knew well enough to conversate with. Her face turned up as she watched Amadeo speak to people and dap them up as if nothing was wrong with him a little while before they arrived. The fakeness that he was displaying made her sick to her stomach.

She knew it was an unwritten rule in the business world that you had to wear many hats to make shit happen. But now, at a moment like this, to be fifty-two fake wasn't appeasing to her. Either he was mourning Trevion, or he wasn't. But to give her the shitty side of him and everyone else the cool as shade side, didn't sit well with her. In fact, it made her even more suspicious of him. She hated to think he was cheating, but why else would he be acting weird towards her. It didn't make sense.

As she continued to observe the scene, a bit of annoyance filled her space. The way people were talking and carrying on, one would think it was a social hour rather than a grieving time. The smiles, laughter, and joking around seemed unfit. They were all supposed to support Royelle and help her through this, but the way it looked and sounded said something completely different.

AJ wanted to separate herself from the crowd. She wondered who everyone was. Were they Trevion's friends, Royelle's friends, family, or a combination of all? She didn't know. Nevertheless, they were all too loud and obnoxious, Amadeo included, and AJ wanted no parts of it. She desperately wanted to march up the stairs to see Royelle, but that theory quickly escaped her, knowing that doing so would've caused many eyebrows to rise.

When she heard a door slam from the upstairs level, she turned towards the noise, only to be beauty struck when she spotted Royelle tailing behind Xandra down the stairs. She couldn't help but stare. She was shocked to see Royelle looking the way she was. She didn't look like someone in mourning or someone who had been in an accident suffering from any form of amnesia.

Her hair was pulled back into a slick ponytail, and her makeup was subtle yet noticeable. She had on her diamond-studded earrings, a black lace bodysuit with a white camisole underneath, black fitted yoga-type pants, black heeled riding boots, and her wedding ring could blind anyone within a three-mile radius.

To everyone in the house, she looked well put together, refreshed and unbothered, and conducted herself as such. By the time she made it halfway down the stairs, anyone who knew anything about scents knew she was wearing Jo Malone's Nectarine Blossom and Honey perfume. She looked and smelled great. AJ was glad to see that no one would have the glory in saying that Royelle had let herself go or that Trevion had destroyed her. She had shown the strengths of a well-kept woman, and it was a complete turn-on for AJ.

"What's up, AJ." Xandra nodded her head.

AJ quickly looked around to see if Amadeo was within earshot. He didn't know anything about her nickname, and to hear it now would not have been conducive. However, AJ relaxed when she saw that the coast was clear. Xandra noticing AJ's worrying disposition, chuckled a little bit. The thought of Amadeo finding out AJ's true identity didn't phase her the least bit.

When Royelle made it to the bottom of the stairs, she excitedly wrapped her arms around AJ and squeezed her as if it was the last hug they would ever share; AJ returned the gesture. Royelle felt so good, warm, and delicate. She smelled sweet enough to eat and looked amazing. AJ didn't want to let her go.

"It's you again!" Royelle smiled. "How long have you been here?" Royelle asked, releasing her grip from around AJ.

"Not too long. How are you feeling, though?" AJ quickly changed the subject.

"I'm getting through, you know. One day at a time, as they say. But, give me a second. I'll be right back."

Royelle walked away and went towards the family room, where most of the other guests were hanging out, and began greeting everybody. She merely wanted to get it all out of the way so that she could put all her focus back into AJ.

"So, what's going on AJ," Xandra asked while keeping her eye on Royelle.

"Not much. Just here to show my support."

"I hear you. I see you're here with company." She indistinctly pointed at Amadeo.

"Yea. He wanted to be here for moral support, you know."

"Mmm-hmm. I'm sure. Is that what he said, or are you saying that?" She queried.

"What do you mean?"

Xandra sucked her teeth. "Nothing." She cut her eyes over at AJ and pressed her lips together. "So, how things been with y'all since that fight y'all had?"

"Quiet. And now that Trevion's gone, I'll never get the truth."

"Ohhh, I wouldn't count the truth out just yet."

"Why do you say that? Do you know something I don't know? AJ questioned.

"Nah, I don't. But, as they say. The truth always comes out, right? And if there's anything that you're supposed to know, stop looking for it and watch how it finds you."

"I guess you're right," AJ responded.

"Mmm-hmmm. I know."

AJ cracked a smile as she and Royelle quickly locked and released their visual grip. AJ was simply captivated by Royelle. She wanted her so bad. Not just sexually, but as a complete package. She saw herself in a future with Royelle. Their sex was great, but the intimacy they shared was greater. Of course, no one else knew, but their chemistry was magnetic. Every time they were around each other, they felt the other one's vibes and equally hated the times they had to share with others. Today was one of those times. When Xandra saw the nonverbal interaction between Royelle and AJ, she smiled. Seeing her sister at peace was all the joy she needed. And as much as she hated to admit it, a part of her liked AJ for her sister.

"Aye. Keep an eye on our girl. Like I told you before, sometimes she forgets what she's doing and why she's doing it. But, I'll be right back." Xandra said

She walked into the kitchen with all intents and purposes of getting an up-close look at Amadeo. She knew what he looked like from a distance, but she wanted to see him. Smell him. Hear him. Get a feel for him. It was almost like a lion hunting its prey. She wanted to learn him. She had to learn him. From the moment she caught him and Trevion together, she hated him as much as she hated Trevion. Although she didn't know how long it was going on between them, she knew the affair they had was incomprehensible and way deeper than the one Royelle was having with AJ. She didn't care that she had a double-standard view about the affairs. In her eyes, the affair between Royelle and AJ would've never happened had Trevion not introduced her sister into his world from the beginning.

"What's going on, fellas?" She said, walking up on Amadeo and Raymelle.

"What's up, sis?" Raymelle responded.

"Funny, I had no idea Royelle had other sisters." Amadeo chimed in.

"And you are?" Xandra clapped back, playing dumb.

"My apologies. I'm Amadeo, Ajah's husband."

"Husband, huh?" Xandra looked him up and down with a stank face. "I didn't know AJ had a husband." She purposely said. "So, we're even."

"Mannn, bro. Don't pay her no mind. She's like that with everybody." Raymelle said.

"I'm not worried about her." Amadeo laughed in amusement.

"Oh, but you should be. I'm a force to be reckoned with." Xandra smirked as she began walking away.

"By the way, her name is Ajah."

Xandra stopped and turned back towards him. "Say again?"

"My wife. Her name is Ajah, not AJ."

"If you say so." Xandra chucked the deuces and walked away.

In those two minutes, she learned he was a weak, misogynistic man who wanted to be in control, and he was nosey as fuck. But it made sense to her since she saw him as a bottom feeder, a man who took it but didn't give it.

"Are you ok?" Royelle walked up to AJ and asked.

"I should be asking you that." AJ responded.

Royelle answered yes, as they began to talk and watch guest after guest come and go. It was a revolving door, and Royelle couldn't wait for it to be over. She may have appeared normal like everyone else; however, she was anything but. The persistent blockage of Trevion and all the events surrounding him consumed every ounce of her. She wanted so badly to know everything there was to know about him without pretending to know or being forced to remember. To her, it seemed like a roller coaster ride with no end. She not only wanted her memories of Trevion back, but she also needed them so she could heal and move on.

Despite him being absent from her mind, body, and spirit, she was glad that her vision was clear about how good AJ always made her feel. She didn't trust many people, but she still had needs that needed to be met. And since her spirit grew fuzzy around AJ, that was a clear indication that it was ok. Whatever *it* was.

"Let's go upstairs and talk where it's a little quieter," Royelle asked.

AJ agreed and went into the kitchen to let Amadeo know that Royelle wanted to talk to her privately. But before she could finish getting the words out, Amadeo had pushed past her and rushed over to Royelle, never noticing that Xandra was on his heels.

"Hey, Royelle. How are you?" Amadeo grabbed both of her hands. "I'm really sorry for your loss. Trevion was a great friend. This is a devasting loss for me as well."

"Mmm-hmm. I bet." Xandra muttered under her breath.

Royelle looked at him and thanked him for coming. If Amadeo was expecting more than a thank you, he was sadly mistaken. This wasn't the time or place for any kumbaya moments. Any business talk or awkward conversations down memory lane would have to take a back seat.

Royelle excused herself and let Amadeo know she needed to speak privately with his wife. And although he didn't oppose Royelle's overture, he certainly didn't like the rejected feeling she gave him. Nor did he care too much about the private meeting she wanted to have with AJ upstairs in her room. But, as a man, he would never let his discourse about it show in front of other people, especially women.

"Sis, I'm down here if you need me," Xandra said loudly.

She wanted to be sure that what she said echoed loud enough for Amadeo to hear just in case he got any dumb-ass ideas of marching up the stairs on some stupid shit. He and Xandra went their separate directions in the house while Royelle and AJ continued up the stairs and into the room. When they got inside, Royelle locked the door.

AJ stood in the center of the room looking around, and it was nothing like she remembered it. Now, the room was covered in post-it notes and pictures of her and Trevion. They were all reminders of who he was to her and a way to keep her mind from constantly forgetting. It broke AJ. It was confirmation that Royelle had amnesia, which made AJ feel low. She had never known or seen anyone with amnesia, so to see it in full view attached to the woman she loved made her feel like shit.

"Weird, huh?" Royelle asked, taking note of AJ's surprised look.

AJ honestly didn't know what to say. Although in disbelief at what she was looking at, she was glad she had a front row seat of it. An unknowing mind is an ignorant one. And now that she knew what Royelle was up against, she could understand it a little better. As AJ continued to look at the new wall art of post-it notes, Royelle sat on the bed and began unzipping her boots. She pulled her pants down, unfastened her bodysuit, and pulled her G-string over to the side."AJ, come eat my pussy." She said in a small soft, yet demanding voice.

"Huh?" AJ turned and asked, taken aback by her command and shocked at Royelle's nakedness.

"Huh, isn't what I said. There may be a lot of things I have forgotten, but how you make me feel isn't one of them."

AJ, thrilled to see her pearl in plain view, walked over to Royelle, asked no questions, and dove headfirst in the center of her legs, slowly licking in-between each one of her lips. AJ's tongue was wet, silky, and warm, and her lips were as soft as Royelle remembered them. Most girls that AJ knew liked being sucked on fast with a bit of roughness; Royelle wasn't that girl. She enjoyed being sucked on in a gentle, caressing, and slow manner. Almost like making love to the pussy with your mouth rather than a penis. And if it was done right, the only focus Royelle placed on her thoughts was how good her body was feeling. And AJ never failed to deliver.

AJ slipped two fingers inside of Royelle's wet heat, and Royelle relished in the enjoyment of it all. The more time and pleasure AJ released onto Royelle, the more it connected to every nerve in Royelle's body, causing her brain to release a burst of blurred visions. She didn't know if she wanted AJ to stop or to keep going. She was trying so hard not to switch focuses or turn her attention to the cloudiness of her thoughts, but the force was so strong, she didn't even realize she was no longer moaning or grabbing AJ's head as tight as she once was. At this point, no matter what way AJ's tongue moved or how her fingers stroked, it didn't deter Royelle's focus from trying to zero in on what her mind wanted to remember.

Given Royelle's silence, it was clear to AJ that Royelle was in a different place. Noticing the shift in Royelle's reaction, AJ opened her eyes and watched Royelle's body language and facial expressions closely as she continued to try and passionately pleasure her.

"Hold on, AJ." Royelle gently pushed AJ's head away from her juice box.

"What's wrong? Did I hurt you or something?" AJ got up and gently wiped her mouth.

"Give me a minute."

Royelle grabbed her things and rushed into the bathroom. She quickly washed her front area, got dressed, and unlocked her door before sitting beside AJ. The last thing she needed was assumptions of her and AJ being thrown around. Since this was the first time Royelle had ever rejected AJ in such a way, AJ didn't know what to say. So, she let Royelle take the lead on this one.

"AJ, I'm sorry. You didn't do anything wrong. In fact, you did everything right."

"So, why'd you stop me?" AJ asked.

"This is going to sound weird, but the more you licked and sucked on me, the more I started to see flashes of something. Only I couldn't make out what it was. It was like a dream almost, but there were so many clouds I could only see silhouettes of people and nothing else. No voices, no nothing. Just people in a room. The weird part is, it looked like the silhouettes were having sex."

AJ wondered if the silhouettes that Royelle was referencing could've been her, Trevion, and Royelle during the times they had their threesomes. She wondered if her eating Royelle somehow contributed to Royelle regaining a little of her memory, and it frightened AJ a bit.

"Ok. So, is that a good thing or a bad thing? Cause I can keep going, you know. Maybe we can break through those clouds." AJ joked.

"It's neither, really. It makes me uncomfortable because whatever is going on with me clearly hinders everything else. Look at me. I can't even enjoy sex if I wanted to." She sadly said.

AJ grabbed her hand. "Or maybe you're just not ready, Royelle. Your body may need more time to process all of this, and that's ok." AJ hugged her and didn't release the hold until Xandra barged into the room.

"Ayeee! What y'all got going on up in here?" She laughed.

"Ewww sis! Business? Get you some." Royelle joked.

"You know, ever since you came out of that coma, you been acting real ghetto. Let me find out that bump on your head opened up a side we ain't ready for." Xandra laughed. "But, nahhh. I came up here because you're being summonsed." She pointed at AJ.

"Me? By who?"

"Who else? You don't think you that important up in here, do you?" Xandra laughed.

"Sis, be nice." Royelle smiled.

"I am being nice damnnnn! I'm just joking. AJ knows that. I mean Ajah." Xandra giggled.

"I'm sure he doesn't want much of anything. But I'mma go ahead and go. I'll call you later." AJ kissed Royelle on the cheek and left out.

"So, what y'all was doing up in here? Xandra pressed.

Royelle didn't answer. She wanted to keep that experience to herself. She found it would be more fitting to share with whatever therapist she would seek help from. There were just some things Xandra couldn't understand, and Royelle was in no position to explain it to her. Since Royelle wasn't going to spill the beans about her private meeting with AJ, Xandra pointed at Royelle's journal and told her not to forget to read it. Tomorrow was a big day, and she needed Royelle in full gear. When Xandra walked out of the room, Royelle opened it up and began reading page after page. As soon as she was done, she had no questions about the next day's activities. She snatched a piece of paper out of her journal and began writing her speech.

CHAPTER 22:
BIRDS OF A FEATHER

*T*he saying birds of a feather flock together may have been actual in some instances, but Bella hated this new idea that Aruba hatched up for the three of them. And after the harsh words and two slaps that Aruba delivered to Bella's face some days prior, Bella didn't want shit to do with her and dreaded having to deal with her today. But she had no choice. Today's agenda was already planned and set in motion from the time Aruba saw Trevion's death notification in the Metro.

Bella thought of all the ways and reasons she could back out of it, but nothing good enough came to mind. Since Aruba knew too much of her business and her movements, it made it impossible for her to come up with a reason as to why she couldn't be where she needed to be today. Therefore, she sucked it up, found something to wear, and went ahead to prepare for a day of Aruba's unwanted bullshit.

It wasn't enough that she was caught on camera and the potential suspect of two murders, but she was sure Aruba would've killed her or ordered a hit on her by now for getting her caught up with Jayson. But Bella knew Aruba wasn't stupid. She was dumb in many regards, but knowing how the police operate wasn't one of them. Bella knew if any harm would've met her after Aruba got questioned by Jayson, all arrows would've pointed directly at her. And, it wasn't a heat that Aruba was ready to sweat in.

Aruba never told Bella the extent of what Jayson asked or said, but it was clear after Aruba's encounter with him, she didn't want shit to do with Bella. She not only stopped calling her, hanging with her, or inviting her over, she also stopped supplying her with clients. And just as simple as that, Bella's pockets became dry.

When Aruba finally called Bella to tell her about her plan to attend the memorial service, Bella wanted nothing to do with it. She was a fucked up person, no doubt, for fucking with Trevion on the side knowing he was married to Royelle, but to show up at his memorial service and sit in his wife's face was a different level of disrespect that Bella just didn't vibe with.

But it was either that or deal with Aruba's wrath. Bella chose the memorial service. Until she could figure out another game plan and how to get from under Aruba's grip, she was going to have to play ball. She was finally dressed and began the fifteen-minute drive to Aruba's apartment, with Trevion being the only thing on her mind. She loved everything about him. And although she was his employee, he treated her special. Unlike Aruba and McKenzie, Bella needed for nothing so long as she continued to see him whenever and however he wanted out of the sights of Aruba and Royelle.

She giggled as she reminisced about the last good fuck session they had when they almost got caught by Royelle. The memory of Trevion making her hit her face while fucking her from the back made her burst out into laughter. She had never seen someone so afraid of headlights shining through a living room window before. And it was moments like that, that made her heart flutter. The excitement of knowing he wanted her, and she wanted him, but couldn't do it openly is what she thrived off.

In the same manner, it saddened her to know that, that time and place would be the last time she would see him or hear his voice again. The idea that he was no longer in the picture was devasting. He was the one person who kept her grounded. And now, with him gone, she had dumb ass Aruba to deal with on a consistent basis, and that wasn't going to work.

Trevion, making Aruba in charge of the girls was one of the biggest mistakes he could've made. Things might've not been so bad had Aruba at least tried to take the incentive to run the game as Trevion did, but she didn't. She took her title literally and treated everyone under her like shit, forgetting she was in their exact position at one point in time with more miles ran on her pussy than Bella's and McKenzie's combined. She wanted so badly to be a boss, where the title didn't fit.

"Don't these niggas ever get tired of just fucking sitting here?" Bella mumbled as she pulled up to the building.

She was so sick and tired of seeing the same tired ass niggas on the steps doing the same tired ass thing; nothing. Finally, when she got out of the car and began walking towards the building, the chattering sounds of the dudes could be heard. *'Oh, god!'* She thought. She just wanted to get in the building without the bullshit that always followed them.

"You ain't in no hurry today, I see." One of the dudes said.

"Nope. Just trying to get upstairs to my sis's crib."

"Oh, yea? That's what's up. You can go though." He licked his lips while undressing her with his eyes. "You a fine piece of ass, you know that?" He continued, but she ignored him.

She was a fine piece of ass, but not one any of them could afford. She paced herself and slowly took her time going up each flight of stairs. When she made it to Aruba's, she knocked on the door, and McKenzie answered.

"Heyyy girllll! Been waiting on you."

"Hey, what's going on?" Bella responded in a toned-down voice.

She walked in, went straight to the living room, sat on the couch, and started scrolling through her phone. It was all a ploy to avoid conversation with McKenzie and keep the peace with Aruba, who was still in her room getting dressed.

McKenzie was happy to see Bella and wanted to kick it with her, but picking up on her low-grade attitude, she decided against it. She grabbed her phone and began doing the same thing Bella was doing—scrolling through social media bullshit. The living room was quiet. No one said a word. McKenzie couldn't figure out what Bella's problem was. And likewise, Bella didn't know what, if anything, McKenzie knew about the last time she was there or about Aruba getting questioned by Jayson.

Unfortunately, Bella's assumptions caused tension in a room where tensions weren't necessary. McKenzie was oblivious to those events as she was to just about everything else happening around her.

"Today's the day bitches! Are y'all ready?!" Aruba yelled, walking into the living room.

McKenzie and Bella both nodded their heads yes.

"All right. Well, we already talked about this, but just to remind y'all. We go there and act normal. Don't be overdoing shit. We don't want to stand out like sore thumbs."

"Don't you think you might?" McKenzie asked.

"How you figure that?" Aruba frowned.

"Well, cause she don't know you."

"She don't know that bitch either," Aruba said, pointing at Bella. "So, what's the difference?"

"You're right. But you got on a fur she doesn't." McKenzie giggled.

"Oh, yea! That would make a difference, huh?!" Aruba laughed and quickly took it off. "Now, back to what the fuck I was saying."

Bella had tuned Aruba out well before she even started talking. She wasn't feeling her at all. She starred at Aruba as she spoke, but it was like she was looking through her instead of at her. Her words could be heard but comprehending them was another thing. As far as Bella was concerned, Aruba was public enemy number one, and there wasn't shit she was could say that would interest her.

"Helloooo! Earth to Belle! Did you hear any of what the fuck I just said?" Aruba questioned.

"I shook my head, yea." Bella shot back.

"You know what, let me talk to you." Aruba harshly said.

She stormed off to her room, and Bella followed behind. McKenzie couldn't understand why Aruba had to take the conversation in the room to begin with. The apartment was small, and the walls were thin. Anything being discussed could be heard clear as day. It was almost as if the conversations were happening right in front of her. But to make sure she wasn't missing a beat, as soon as the bedroom door closed, McKenzie tip-toed to the hall to try and get a better listen to what was being said.

"What the fuck is the problem?! Are you still mad about the other day?"

"Ain't nothing wrong, Aruba. I'm fine," Bella responded lowly.

"Don't fucking patronize me, Belle!" She walked up to Bella, roughly grabbing her face.

"I said I'm fineee." Bella attempted to pull her face away, but Aruba grabbed it tighter.

"Then act like it!" Aruba shoved Bella's face away and began to walk out the room but stopped short.

"Do you know the reason you have the money you have? The clients you do? The clout you do? It's because we put you on. We let you into our empire! We helped you build! So, if you can't understand why the fuck I'm so mad about you not following the rules, that's just too fucking bad. Now fix your fucking face, and let's make it."

As soon as McKenzie heard those last words, she hauled her ass back to the couch and submerged her face into her phone, pretending to be on social media like before. When Aruba walked out, Bella stayed behind for a few moments, trying to calm the rage inside her. *'We? Who the fuck is we?'* She thought. She was pissed. All this talk about we, and there was no we. Trevion had always been top dog. He simply gave Aruba some silver, and she tried to turn it into gold. Aruba was nothing but a scram, and the only reason she got any kind of respect was because of Trevion.

But giving her the rank didn't change the fact that she had always been jealous of how hard he cut for Bella, and even in his death, Aruba was still invidious of her. And since Bella knew it, she was gonna use Aruba's discontent and Trevion's death for her benefit. Therefore, rather than responding to all of Aruba's tough talk and abuse, she stayed quiet, keeping her other plans in the back of her mind on how she was going to deal with Aruba later.

Bella fixed herself up, came out of the room, and the three of them left out to Aruba's car. Usually, Bella would be riding shotgun, but the way things were going, she needed to stay away from Aruba at all cost. Bella hopped in the backseat behind the passenger, forcing McKenzie to sit in the front. The ride was quiet. Everybody was in their own frame of mind trying to deal with their own thoughts, and while Bella couldn't wait for it to be over, the other two were anxious to get it started.

"All right y'all. We here. Remember what we talked about."

The ladies didn't say a word. They got out of the car, readjusted their clothes, and put their game faces on. They looked like Toffee, Caramel, and Mocha versions of Charlie's Angels as they walked through the parking lot towards the building. The only thing missing was their Hershey rendition of Bosley.

CHAPTER 23:
THE MEMORIAL SERVICE

lthough Royelle was neither happy nor sad about the memorial service, she couldn't help but give herself kudos for all she had done on her own. She not only booked the Scranton Hall, but she also contacted the Boston Herald, Boston Globe, and The Metro. For her having Trevion's memorial service publicized was imperative to the plan. Once she was able to make contact with each individual that headed the death notices in the local papers, she paid the required fee for each and gave them the date and city of death, details of the public memorial service, surviving family members, in-laws, including herself as the wife, their unborn child, with an added inscription that read:

"Every man deserves a great woman by her side. I'm so glad and honored to say that you chose me for the past five years. Of the billions of women in the world; your heart, mind, and soul has always set its shine upon me. It has been such an amazing five-year journey and one that ended way too soon. I'm so sorry you won't be here physically to meet our little one, but I know you'll be with us every step of the way spiritually. I love you, Trevion, and will miss you deeply. See you one day soon on the other side. Love your one and only wife, Royelle Kingsley."

Once she knew that the notice would be printed for a week, she was ecstatic, knowing that it was going to reach the masses even if she couldn't. Word traveled fast in the land of fuckery and bullshit. So, she knew that a friend was going to tell a friend who would tell another friend, who she was hoping was connected to the secret wife.

Frankly, she was pretty emotionless and couldn't care less about having his memorial service. The more she learned and journaled about him, the more generated hate she gained for him. All the good things that people told her about him were what she called his *"characters in shadows."* Those were the masks he wore so that the outside world wouldn't recognize or see the real him. In Royelle's heart, the true him was the one that Xandra continued to obliterate.

Royelle kept reading her notes, and the more she read, the dumber she began to feel for having the memorial service. Here it was a few weeks since she had been home, and she was no closer to learning anything more about his death or the so-called other wife. It plagued her that she could have been so stupid and blind not to see the signs of him living a double life. But she vowed not to let his fallacies become any of her realities.

"Welcome, Ladies. Please sign in before going inside." The usher directed the trio.

One by one, they each signed in and went through the second set of double doors that led them into Scorpion Landing's function room.

"Hello. Please be seated anywhere you like," another usher said while handing them a program and memorial card.

Trying to get a feel for the room, they looked around at all the other guests as they slowly walked towards the first available table they saw. When they took their seats, it was clear to them that Trevion was much more liked and respected than either of them had given him credit for.

As much as Aruba and McKenzie hated to admit it, it was also evident that Royelle did everything with class, style, and taste. Regardless of the event being buffet-style, the place was dipped to the nines. She was not playing about the appearance she was trying to portray for all those in attendance. Everybody knew her as Trevion's sophisticated, fashionable, and dignified wife, and that's how she wanted her image to remain once everything was all said and done.

Bella loved every detail that Royelle put into the service. It was easy to see why Trevion was so gun-ho about keeping her at bay, making sure she was straight. Royelle was everything that she and Aruba weren't, and Bella could see it without knowing or having met Royelle.

As Xandra looked on at Royelle, a stronger sense of guilt joined her thoughts. She never thought in a million years Trevion's story would end with her taking his life. At a minimum, she felt the worst that could happen was Royelle learning the truth about him and Amadeo, divorcing his sorry ass, and cleaning him out of everything because of it. But this was way more than anyone, including Xandra, had bargained for. Yet, she still had to do what Xandra had always done for Royelle, and that was to protect her.

"A'ight sis. You good?" Xandra asked. It's almost that time."

"I'm ok," Royelle responded.

"Ohhh-kayyy. I'm gonna be right beside you every step of the way in case you get stuck. But you got your speech right there, ok." Xandra pointed down at Royelle's right hand. "You ready to go out there and greet these folks, see what's what?"

Royelle looked in the mirror, took an abstract look at herself, and stood up.

"I'm ready, sis. You always said we gotta lay cheese to catch a rat, right?"

"Mmm-Hmm. That's exactly what the fuck I said." Xandra smiled.

"Well. Cheese has been laid. Now let's see what we can trap." Royelle responded.

"Okkkkk bitchhhhh!" Xandra excitedly said while smiling big. She was impressed with Royelle's remembrance and comeback.

The two prepared to leave the bridal room suite where they had been getting dressed, sitting, and talking for the last few hours. It was their time to be with each other without the annoyance of others, and it allowed Xandra the opportunity to get Royelle's mind right for what was to come. But once Royelle opened the door and heard all the chatter coming from the function room, she tensed up.

"Roy? You good?" Xandra asked.

Royelle didn't respond.

"Royelle?" Xandra called her name again.

"I'm ok, sis. I'm ok. Just trying to process."

"We can go back inside until you're ready. Fuck these people. They'll just have to wait."

"It's ok, sis. I can do this." Royelle reaffirmed.

She closed her eyes, took a deep breath through her nose, and exhaled it out of her mouth as she reopened her eyes. Then, with Xandra following closely behind, she began walking into the function room, and suddenly all the chatter went silent. It was like giving someone a standing ovation but in a different form.

"There goes the woman of the hour," Aruba sneered.

She had an ingratiating disdainful look on her face as her eyes followed every direction Royelle moved. The sight of her looking like an angel was gut-wrenching for Aruba. Royelle's all-white one-piece, skinny pencil romper jumpsuit, with an attached train, gave off the illusion of angel wings blowing every time she took a step. Her look made Aruba and McKenzie breed with hate. Bella, however, followed with lust in her eyes at her beauty. *'She should've been my sister-wife from the start.'* Bella thought as she continued to lay her eyes on Royelle.

Her overall appearance, hair, and makeup included were flawless. She was simply stunning. Even AJ and Amadeo, who were in attendance, couldn't keep their eyes off of her. And no matter how much Aruba and McKenzie wanted to hate her, there was no refuting her radiance.

"What do you wanna do first," Xandra whispered.

"I guess we can go around and start greeting people until we get started."

"Lead the way, sis. I'm right behind you."

Naturally, Xandra would've been against it. Royelle was the one in mourning, so it should've been them coming to her, not the other way around. But since they were on a different type of mission, Xandra was all for it. Table by table, Royelle and Xandra began making their rounds throughout the room, shaking everyone's hands and thanking them for coming.

Xandra was very strategic in having the photographers take pictures of everything and everyone, even if they didn't know they were being photographed. There was a plan in motion, and so far, it was working out just the way Xandra saw it planned out in her head. By the time they made it to the 5th table out of the ten that were set up, a tap on the microphone interrupted their flow.

"Good afternoon, everyone."

As soon as Royelle and Xandra heard Raymelle's voice, they knew it was time to be seated. They hurried to the other side where their reserved table was, and Royelle sat down in front of Raymelle while Xandra remained standing off to the side.

"Thank you all for coming out today. On behalf of my sister and Trevion's wife Royelle, myself, the Blevins, and the Kingsley family, we are truly grateful to have you here. Thank you for your continued support during this difficult time. Trevion was a great man, loved and liked by so many. Unfortunately, we cannot celebrate him in the way that we truly want to, but we are going to celebrate him in the way my sister best sees fit." Raymelle looked over at Royelle. " This is dope, sis. Trevion would be so pleased. Great job! Salud!" He raised his glass.

Raymelle continued with his speech down memory lane while Royelle read hers, trying to prepare for her turn. Xandra, looking like security, was attempting to memorize all the faces she didn't know and acknowledged all the ones she did. She wasn't a very friendly person, but for the sake of answers, she had to be a different her, and she hated it.

"This nigga tired. He's wearing me the fuck out with all his talk. I'm ready to go," Aruba whispered to the other two.

Bella nor McKenzie responded. They didn't even look her way. And even though they knew her reasoning for being there, they still felt her temperament was disrespectful, and she was about to expose them by moving too fast. Getting up in the middle of the speech to leave out was not a good move to make. Therefore, they pretended like they didn't hear what she said and continued to listen to Raymelle as he welcomed Royelle and gracefully extended his hand out to guide her up to the podium. Xandra, as usual, was trailing, right behind her.

"Aye. Who's the bitch that keeps following her around," Aruba whispered to the girls.

"I think that's her sister," McKenzie whispered back.

"Hmph. Ok"

Aruba took out her phone and started taking pictures of Royelle and Xandra while unknowingly having her photos being taken by the photographer.

"Good Afternoon, everybody."

"Good afternoon," The guest responded in harmony.

"Thank you all for being here. My brother said an earful didn't he." Everyone laughed.

As Royelle continued talking, her voice began to sound like Charlie Brown's wah, wah, wah, wah, wah, vocabulary to Aruba. Her blood welled with a scornful detestation towards Royelle. Being in the same room with her was hard enough. But listening to her sweet, soft voice, observing her absolute beauty, witnessing the love and respect they all had for her and Trevion's seemingly perfect relationship made her feel repelled. Everything Royelle was and had was everything she lacked.

"My husband was simply amazing. He made sure that I needed for nothing. And everything I didn't even know I needed or wanted, he gave me. Spoiled? Yes!"

Those words snapped Aruba out of her cloud of thoughts. Hearing what Royelle was saying about her and Trevion's relationship made her feel some kind of way. What Trevion told her about the relationship and the reason for him being in it versus what Royelle was saying wasn't adding up. It sounded to Aruba like Trevion was much more in love with Royelle than he led anyone in their circle to believe.

Aruba was so hung up on what Royelle was saying and how she was looking that she didn't even realize she was making her low-profile a known profile to an eagle-eye Xandra. She had already noticed them looking like three top-paid hoes when she walked into the function room. And from that moment, she kept a guarded eye on them.

Royelle finished her speech, thanked everyone, and invited them to the buffet as they enjoyed the slide show Xandra put together. But before she could say or do anything else, Xandra hurried her away from the podium when she noticed the three musketeers preparing to leave.

"Sis. What are you doing?" Royelle asked confusingly.

"Hush. Just roll with me on this and act normal. Cause these bitches are about to leave."

"Whooo, sis?" Royelle asked, confused.

"Hello, ladies. How y'all doing," Xandra asked with a fake smile draped across her face.

"Hey, McKenzie. What are you doing here? I mean, thank you for being here, but you're the last person I would've expected to see here. Who are your friends?" Royelle asked.

"This is Aruba."

"Aruba? That's different." Xandra reacted.

"Yes. I know. It means *'loves her husband'* in Muslim." She arrogantly responded.

Xandra giggled.

"Why's that funny," Aruba questioned Xandra.

"No reason. It just is."

"And you are?" Royelle asked.

"Isabel," Bella answered in a soft voice.

She stuck her hand out to shake Royelle's, and Royelle was more than happy to do so.

"And who are you since you questioning and clowning on me?" Aruba asked.

Xandra chortled. "Sis. They call me sis."

Aruba extended her hand to shake Xandra's.

"Oohhh chileeee. Na-uh." Xandra quickly put her hands behind her back. "I don't shake hands, honey. Imma big germ-a-phobe. You understand." Xandra responded in the most gayest-uppity-bougiest-*I'm a queen, and to good for your peasant ass* voice that she could make. "Well, now that we got all the greetings out of the way. I just wanted Royelle to come over and say hello because I saw that y'all were getting ready to go." Xandra continued.

"So, besides McKenzie, how do you all know Trevion?" Royelle asked.

Xandra was shocked to hear Royelle's question. She didn't think Royelle would know to ask such a thing, but she was sure glad she did. Xandra smiled big as she waited on their response.

"We didn't know him personally. We're just here in support of McKenzie, who came to support you."

"Well, that was very kind of you all. Especially since I know McKenzie barely even knew him." Royelle said.

McKenzie gave a look of revulsion.

"Nevertheless, thank you. Are you ladies sure you don't want to stay for food?" Royelle asked.

"No, we're good. We just wanted to come pay our respects." Aruba replied.

"Well, don't let us hold y'all. Enjoy the rest of the night, and thank y'all for coming." Xandra said.

Xandra took mental notes of the whole encounter. From the way, Aruba spoke to the way the other two remained quiet with their heads slightly hanging low. It was a classic pimp's and hoe's game that Xandra was all too familiar with. But, in her heart of hearts, she knew that somehow one of them was directly connected to Trevion's other wife in one way or another. And finding out who was now part of her mission.

"Who the fuck was that?! And what the fuck was her problem," Aruba yelled, walking back towards her car. "Bitch don't shake hands?! Like I really wanted to shake hers. Ole raggedy ass bitch!" Aruba continued.

"I knew that was her sister from the pictures at the office, but I'm sure sis ain't her name," McKenzie said.

"Yea! No shit! Sherlock!" Aruba snapped.

McKenzie lowered her head and didn't say shit else. She felt stupid for trying to fit in where there wasn't any room for her. Bella just stayed quiet. She didn't look any particular way, and she didn't respond to anything.

Aruba went through her phone's photo gallery to look at the pictures she got of Xandra and Royelle, and they were of perfect quality. It gave her an adrenaline rush, just thinking about the moment she'd be able to unleash her dragon onto them. She was heated. She felt disrespected, which never happened, especially not in front of her workers. Xandra didn't only undermine her authority persona, but she also made her feel like she had just been punked. And for that, Xandra was gonna have to pay, not privately, but publically. She needed Xandra to feel the same humiliation that she did.

"So where to now," McKenzie asked.

"Nowhere. Imma drop y'all off. I got some shit to handle."

Bella badly wanted to know what the fuck she was up to, and had it not been for her recent fuck up with Jayson, she would have known. Of course, she couldn't be one hundred percent sure that whatever Aruba was up to had anything to do with Xandra, but her intuition wouldn't let her feel anything different.

"This might not be any of my business—"

"So, why even bother going any further. If you're starting the shit off like that, Belle, then it ain't your business, now is it?" Aruba cut in.

'Ooohhh! I just wanna smack this bitch!' Bella thought before responding. "Well, I won't know if it's my business or not till I ask?" Bella sassed.

"What is it, Belle?" Aruba snapped.

"Does what you gotta do have anything to do with that sis bitch?"

"See, I was right— it ain't none of your business. You're on a need-to-know basis. If I need you, I know where to find you, trust me."

Bella wanted to reach over and smash Aruba through the driver's side window. The way she spoke to her and treated her was enough to make any woman violent, and at this point, Bella was having homicidal thoughts about Aruba. She was just waiting for the right time. When they finally pulled up at Aruba's, Bella wasted no time getting out of the car and power walked to her own with McKenzie following right behind.

"Why do you keep letting her talk to you like that?" McKenzie asked, catching up to Bella.

"McKenzie, it's a long story. Just leave it alone." Bella responded as she got into her car.

"No! We got time. What the fuck is going on?"

Bella started her engine while releasing a huge sigh.

"Look. Long story short, I fucked up. They caught me on tape coming in and out of daddy's house, and now I'm somehow linked to his murder and the neighbors."

"Are you fucking serious?! What the fuck were you doing there?!"

"He fucking called me there! He always wanted private sessions. Fuck was I supposed to do, say no?!"

"Well, did you at least tell Aruba?"

"And say what, McKenzie? Hey Aruba, your husband wants to fuck me tonight and every other night without you. You good with that?!" Bella rolled her eyes. "Come on, McKenzie! Think!" Bella pointed at her temple.

"Think?! Think about what? Yes! You should have told her. She is in charge, you know."

"Oh, ok, genius! So, let me guess. You told her about the flowers he sent you to the office or all the times he fucked you in his truck, at the construction sites, at Amadeo's office, in Royelle's office, and without her or me, right?"

McKenzie didn't say a word. She was shocked that Bella knew all of those details. She had no idea that her business with Trevion was leaked. As far as she knew, they were privately intimate, and that's how she liked it. She was wrong.

"I didn't think so! Oh, what? You're surprised that I know all of that. Don't be. I know a whole lot more than you and her think."

"Look! My situation was different from yours." McKenzie tried to downplay.

"How bitch?! Do tell!"

"I was set up to work at her job for a reason, and I had to play my part. Part of that was accepting the flowers, taunting her in the office, going through all her financial documents, and fucking him in the process. But I'm guessing you already knew that."

"It doesn't even matter. Bottom line is, Aruba doesn't know that either of us had been fucking Trevion for as long as we were, and now this fucking tape is out, and I had to make up some bullshit lie as to why I was there."

McKenzie didn't know what to say. They were both in violation of Aruba's rules. But who were they to say no to him? Trevion was their boss, their daddy. He took rank, and what he said went— and when he called or demanded, they obliged, always.

CHAPTER 24:
NEW YORK, NEW YORK

*I*t was nothing for a Bostonian to take a trip to New York on a weekly basis. All you had to do was blast some music, smoke some weed, know all the hot spots statey's frequented, and you were good. And since Aruba was a regular commuter, she had no worries. She pulled over at the first fully functional rest stop she saw on the Mass Pike, got out, stretched her legs, and grabbed her gym bag out of the trunk of the car. She smiled as she walked to the ladies' room to change her clothes into something much more comfortable. Although it had been a minute since she had been to New York, she couldn't have been happier to be on her way there tonight.

Before returning to her car, she picked up some snacks, a few things to drink, and paid to fill up her tank. Her car was good on gas, so the next stop wouldn't be until she made it to Brooklyn. And although happy to be going, the three-and-a-half-hour ride didn't come without a cannonade of questions and doubts. The more she learned about Royelle, the less she felt she knew about Trevion. She thought she knew all there was to know about his mock relationship with Royelle and the money he stood to inherit, but it was all still unclear. She remembered the day he told her about getting caught by Royelle when he was looking for the wills and wondered if her forged signatures on

Royelle's will would still guarantee her a payout.

Things had changed so much with Trevion before he died that it was hard for Aruba to know where she stood in the mix of all the bullshit. The idea was for Trevion to meet Royelle, learn about her pockets, and treat her well so that he could get in. Falling in love with her was not a part of the plan. But here it was, five years into it, and Aruba was learning more about Royelle than Trevion ever verbalized. And for a nigga who didn't so-call love a woman, she couldn't tell. It seemed to Aruba that Trevion had fallen deeper for Royelle than he ever had with any other woman, her included.

She couldn't understand how a nigga of his caliber could dive in headfirst and not come up for air. Royelle, as far as she could tell, had it all. A nice house, car, great job, beautiful, and the one Trevion did the most for. At the same time, she was turning tricks and slept most of her nights in her project apartment on the fourth floor. It didn't seem right. She thought about what Royelle said about being pregnant, and she instantly became inflamed. She replayed the image of Royelle in her White semi-bodycon romper at the memorial service and couldn't recall seeing a baby bump. But that was neither here nor there. The idea of Royelle possibly being pregnant is one of the many things that plagued her.

Of all the times she wanted and tried to get pregnant by Trevion, it never happened. Even when she tried to trick him on the nights when he was fucked up past the point of sobriety, he still remembered to wear protection. And when she asked him why he never fucked her raw, he always reminded her that girls in her profession weren't allowed to get pregnant; otherwise, it fucked up the flow of money.

Truth was, Trevion didn't see Aruba as the mothering type. She was too reckless, couldn't stay out of jail, was on and off drugs, and only wanted to get pregnant to trap him. He knew the game with her. If she was going to mother any child or web any nigga, it wasn't going to be him. Now Royelle and Bella, that was a different story, but he was never ready, and Royelle was never pregnant.

Even McKenzie, with her dumb ass, thought that she was worthy of his sperm count, but he only fucked her to keep her happy, in line, and to make her feel like part of the team. Fact was, she was useless at this point. Hell, she was useless way before Trevion's doom. Trevion thought getting her in the door at Premier would help him learn more about Royelle and her inheritance, but instead of befriending Royelle, all McKenzie did was create a wedge between them.

In McKenzie's mind, if she played a little less friendly, it would keep Royelle out of her business and from figuring out that she was the girl Trevion was talking to when Royelle and Trevion first met. But she was trying too hard, and it back-fired. She made it so bad between her and Royelle that now Royelle couldn't stand her, and Xandra hated her twice as much. She had one assignment, and she failed at it miserably. Point, blank, and simple.

It seemed to Aruba that all the plans she, McKenzie, and Trevion had cooked up against Royelle had crumbled. McKenzie failed to do her due diligence. Aruba was too busy trying to play the boss bitch that she didn't recognize her man had fallen for someone else. And Trevion was so hell-bent on dealing with Amadeo, and the niggas from Xclusive, that he didn't realize his square wife was becoming more street smart day by day.

Bella never knew about any of the deceitful plans that the other three had devised. There were just certain things Trevion didn't want her involved in, and this happened to be one of them. The one and only constant conversation that Trevion had with Bella regarding Royelle was to make her Royelle's sister-wife, and Bella was all for it.

When Aruba finally made it to 1825 Ocean Ave in Brooklyn, she was ecstatic. It didn't take her much to figure out which building she was supposed to be going to; it stood out like a sore thumb. It honestly looked like a piece of a puzzle that didn't belong amongst the other pieces. Every building, except for 1825, was either a Beige, Tan, or a Brick color. 1825 was Cream with Brown window panelings and fancy balconies to match.

"I didn't expect anything less," Aruba said as she drove up closer to the building, looking for parking, and when she couldn't find any, she called upstairs.

"Yo!" The male voice answered.

"It's Aruba. There's no parking on the street. What should I do?"

"Go through the gate. The code is 111316. Park in space OC21.

Aruba did as she was told and found the space three steps away from the doors leading to the front lobby where the elevators were. It was the first time at the new digs, so she couldn't wait to see it all. The outside of the building already had her awestruck. But when she stepped inside of the lobby, she was enthralled with its modern vibrance, style, and comfort.

The pristine attention to detail brought out the marble tiling and oak paneling in the hallways and common spaces, while the pleasant smell of potpourri embraced the atmosphere. Aruba was amazed. She never thought in a million years she would walk into any building in Brooklyn that could carry so much class. When she hopped the elevator, the ride was so smooth that she didn't realize she was moving until she stopped on the 8th floor. Once she made it to unit 8J, D' was already at the door, waiting for her to come in.

"Heyyy D-Rock!" She reached in and hugged him.

"What's up?" He hugged her back.

He opened the door a little wider so she could step in.

"This shit is niceeee! I see y'all living comfortably and shit! That's what's up."

She looked around the two-bedroom condo-style unit in awe at how dope it was and questioned why she was staying in that raggedy-ass project apartment that Whitey Bulger once took rank in. The condo came complete with spacious bedrooms that provided perfect views of the city, a large kitchen, breakfast bar island, stainless steel appliances, central ac and heat, a private rooftop terrace, and laundry room for people who didn't already have a washer and dryer of their own.

There was a co-work space lounge for people who needed to work from home but wanted to leave their home space to inhabit society. There was a full gym, a lounge for residents, complete with pool tables and arcade games, a furnished rooftop deck, bike storage for bicyclists, and paid private parking if you wanted it. 1825 was the shit as far as Aruba was concerned. The only things missing were a bar, a club, and a muthafucking butler.

"You done gazing, Lyra?"

Aruba quickly turned around.

"Da'Vegassss! How are you feeling, honey?" She brought her tone down, walked over, and kissed him on the cheek. "You look really good."

"Ahh! You know. Can't keep a nigga down for too long." He slightly smiled. "How was the drive?"

Da'vegas was making small talk. He really didn't want Aruba at his shit. No matter how long he knew her, he could only tolerate her for so long. But when she called and told him she needed to get away for a moment and needed to talk to him in person, he figured it was something important.

"The drive was straight. As always. Just thinking, smoking, and driving, that's all."

"That shit happened today, didn't it?" Da'Vegas asked.

"What shit? The memorial service?"

"Yea. How was it?"

Aruba laughed.

"Fuck's so funny, Lyra?" Da'Vegas's tone quickly changed.

"I mean, it was alright, I guess."

"You guess? You guess what? Man, stop fucking playing with me, Lyra, and answer the fucking question."

By now, Aruba knew Da'Vegas was not feeling her. He was in no playing mood, and having her there for the next twenty-four hours didn't ease his comportment towards her. She knew if she didn't get some act right, his brother and muscle D-Rock was gonna get some act right outta her, and Dee's type of smoke was the kind of smoke no one ever wanted.

"It was nice. Ole girl did a good job. There were at least 100 people there."

"Damn, that was love, huh?" Da'Vegas smiled. "Aight. Before we get into some long-drawn-out bullshit about what's been going on, go take a shower, eat something, and then we can talk. All the shit you need is in the room and bathroom."

"Cool. Thank you, Vegas." She kissed him on the forehead and went on to handle her business. They waited for her to close the door and hear the sounds of the running water before stepping out onto the deck.

"So, what's the word with her, bro?" D-Rock asked.

"Man, fuck if I know. But I don't wanna hear shit about no fucking Royelle unless there's money involved." Da'Vegas said. "Real nigga shit, bro. I'm bout sick of this bitch. Every time a nigga turns around, she whining about some shit. I can't wait for all this shit to be done with, so she can move the fuck around." He continued.

Da'Vegas was unhinged. Aruba was cool and all, but he thought being in New York would give him the escape he needed; he was wrong. Since he been in New York, she made it her business to see him at least once or twice a week. The drive never bothered her. She would leave Boston at three or four in the morning on any given day, get to New York by seven or eight, spend the whole day there and leave at seven or eight at night, making it back to Boston by eleven or twelve depending on traffic.

But those constant visits annoyed him. Every time she showed up, she had something or someone new to talk about. It was never just to check in on him or kick it. There was always drama. Therefore, while ignoring her calls for the last few weeks, he moved to Ocean Blvd and chilled without the constant ramblings of Aruba. But when she kept texting and pressing the issue of needing to see him, he gave in and regrettably shot her the new address.

"Y'all all right out here?" She asked, stepping onto the deck.

"Yea. We good," Da'Vegs answered.

"Where the liquor at?" She giggled.

D-Rock pointed to the area where they kept a stockpile of white and brown liquor. While Aruba fixed herself something to eat and prepared her drinks, Da'Vegas and Dee sat to watch the Basketball game on T.V. They heard Aruba talking to them, but like many other nights, they had tuned her ass out. Often, she'd talk about things that never interested them. Not to mention, they knew what kind of woman she was, and niggas like them had no sympathy or respect for women like her, but hoes had to eat too, and they made sure of that.

"You good now, Lyra?" Da'Vegas asked when she joined them in the living room.

"Yup. Clean, full, and finally relaxed."

"Bet that. So what's going on? What happened?" Da'Vegas wasted no time getting to the meat of the visit; sides weren't essential.

Before responding, she got up, got her phone out of her purse, and opened it to the gallery section. "Who's this?" She put the phone in Da'Vegas's face.

"That's that bitch Xandra! That hoe was at the shindig today?!"

"Yea, that bitch was there! Talking 'bout her name is sis, and tailing old girl like she was her fucking secret service or some shit."

Seeing a picture of Xandra at the memorial service took him over the top. "Look at this shit, bro!" Da'Vegas showed the picture to D-Rock.

What it meant for Da'Vegas was that Xandra was good. All the rumors of her being gone since Trevion died had been put to rest. She was alive and appeared well. The gossip on the street was that she had a vendetta out for Trevion and might've been the one who had killed him. But no one knew for sure. He was into so much shit with so many people, it was hard to say who might've been involved.

Aruba continued to tell him about Xandra's way of acting throughout the service and towards her and the girls. She also told him that she caught wind from McKenzie and the streets that Royellee was suffering from some form of amnesia. None of that interested Da'Vegas. His mind was so wrapped around the idea that Xandra was around and doing her thing that he couldn't focus his thoughts on anything Aruba had to say until the moment she mentioned the word detectives.

"Wait! Run that back! 'The fuck you say about the D-Boys?"

Aruba could see the flames burning in Da'Vegas's eyes. She delighted in it. Her goal was to eliminate the competition, and what better way to do it than to air Bella out. Therefore, she kept on talking to add to the heat. And the more she spoke, the more the combustion of anger built inside of him.

"So, you said one of the new clients Bella's dealing with is a fucking Detective?"

"Yea. They got her on camera coming in and out of the crib. The neighbor was recording everything. When the detective noticed it was her, they met up, and he told her all about it. I don't know. Bella been—"

"Nah! Stop! I don't wanna hear shit else about Bella."

Da'Vegas was taken aback. He knew Bella wasn't involved, but what boiled him red was the idea that she was in any way fucking a detective.

"Who's in charge of operations?" Da'Vegas sternly asked.

"Me," Aruba answered.

"Who gets the calls about the clients?"

"Me."

"Who's supposed to screen clients before a call out?"

"Me."

"So how the fuck did Bella end up with a client who's a cop?!"

Aruba was stunned. She didn't know what to say. Here she was trying to throw Bella under the bus, and it boomeranged. Not once did she consider the fact that Bella and McKenzie having fucked Jayson would be her fault. But it was. She had dropped the ball. She didn't do any of what she was supposed to do, other than to take his call and get his money. Everything in between she was the least bit concerned with, and now it was about to cost them.

Getting yelled at by Da'Vegas didn't do shit but make her hate Bella even more. She just couldn't win with that bitch. And to Aruba, it always seemed like she did everything wrong, and Bella was all so perfect. But Da'Vegas was right. The error fell on her. Now she was going to have to find a way to clean it all up.

"So, let me ask you a question. Why the fuck are you here?" Da'Vegas asked in a deep dark tone.

"Wha-what do you mean?" She stuttered.

"With all the shit that's going on out there, why the fuck are you here? Shouldn't you be doing some mutherfucking damage control right now?"

"Well, that's why I came here to talk to you. I don't know how to handle it. Those decisions were always made by —."

"Listen!" Da'Vegas cut her off. "Things are different now, and you gonna have to move like they are. Do you understand?"

"Yes. I understand." She replied with her head down.

Aruba was saddened and surprised that Da'Vegas was acting the way he was with her. She was expecting a much more inviting response to her being there and for all the information she had just given him. However, it was anything but inviting. She had unwillingly set herself up to be the center of the fuck-ups.

"Look, you got a lot of shit to handle. Go lay the fuck down, get some

sleep, and in the morning, be out. You can't handle shit being around here."
Da'Vegas ordered.

Aruba didn't say a word. She got up, went into the bedroom, and closed the door behind her. Once she hit, the bed she started crying. She hated that she even bothered to take the time to drive to New York. Da'Vegas wasn't the same person. The expectation she had for their visit was not what she received, and it crushed her.

The following day at 5:22 am, Aruba woke up to the smell of Maple Bacon in the air. She smiled at the thought that Da'Vegas may have been over himself and apologetic for his bullshit the night before. She got out of bed and headed to the shower. When she was done getting dressed, she went into the dining room to find a whole spread of bacon, eggs, waffles, fruit, and a mimosa pitcher.

"Oh wowww!" She softly spoke. "You made all of this?"

"Who else?" Da'Vegas answered.

"Thank you. This is nice."

"Look. You got a long ride home. The least I can do is feed you and make sure you got bread in your pockets."

"Well, I appreciate it. Thank you."

The two sat down and ate breakfast while discussing how things were going personally for Da'Vegas. A lot had changed for him since Aruba had seen him last, so she didn't know how to take him, but she enjoyed him. But she had so much she wanted to get off her chest. She had so many questions about Royelle, the pregnancy, the business, money, everything. But unfortunately, he did more talking than listening, switching from one subject to the next she knew better than to ask. Therefore, she eagerly listened and soaked up all the bullshit he was feeding her as being factual. Once they were done eating, Aruba got up, put the plates in the sink, and headed to the room to gather all her things. When she came back out, Da'Vegas was at the front door waiting on her.

"You got everything?" He asked.

"I sure do." She walked up to him and kissed him softly on the lips as he squeezed her ass.

"Still got it, I see." He joked.

"Why wouldn't I?"

Da'Vegas grabbed her hands and looked her square in the eyes.

"Lyra, look—"

"Why do you keep calling me that?" She interrupted.

"Cause that's your fucking name. I'm not calling you some shit you made up to try and play boss. That name is for the others, not me."

Aruba's eyes lowered, and her smile disappeared.

"Like I was saying. This shit. It'll be over soon a'ight. When the timing is right, we 'gon link like we 'pose to. Just chill."

"I know. I just miss you." She replied.

"I miss you too, but just a little while longer."

Lyra smiled.

"I can't wait for that day. But honestly, how are you really feeling?" She asked.

"I'm good, trust me." He said as he readjusted himself in his wheelchair. "It's gonna be a minute, but I'm good. My bro's here, the doctor's call, come by, or whatever, so trust me, I'm good. I just need to know that you're on your shit. And when you can, find out what's really going with Royelle. I need to know if she really got that amnesia shit I keep hearing about. But in order for you to do that, you gotta stay on your shit like I said. "

Lyra bent down to meet Da'Vegas at eye level. "I hear you loud and clear. Just know, I'm on my shit. Been on my shit. You just worry about recovering from all of this, so we can finish what we started, Trevion.

He grabbed her hand, kissed it, and pulled her in closer. "I know the dead don't speak, but don't you ever call me Trevion again. It's Da'Vegas from now. The name Trevion— that shit died when that nigga did. Remember that.

Acknowledgments

Above all things, I thank God for all that is before me. Every day, I wake up and think about those younger than me who have gone before me, and I am grateful for the life he has spared me so far. Without you, Lord, I am and can do nothing. So, thank you for giving me another chance to get this thing called life right. Never perfect, but always striving for better.

To my homie, lover, friend, and counterpart TK, thank you for always being patient with me. I know this writing journey has taken on a form of its own in our marriage, but you have been steadfast and extremely patient with me since the beginning of it all. And when I start to doubt myself, you, my biggest supporter, keeps me afloat. Thank you for all that you do, how you love and care for me, how you support me and protect me. I couldn't have asked for a better Spidey to be in my corner. I'm covered on all sides. Thank you, Bear! #OC214lyfe!

To my Executive Producer still waiting on her 25%, better known as my daughter Kye, thank you, sweetness, for always being available to me when I am struggling with my writer's block and for co-writing the book blurb. Your creative mind has helped dig me out of many writing holes, and I am so grateful. When I make it, I promise you your 25%, and then some will be delivered on a platter. I love you, kid! Thank you for absolutely everything! 😊

To all of my readers, your patience has been phenomenal! Thank you for trusting in my work and knowing that the wait was worth it. I know it took a while to come through with Book 2, but great work takes time. And even with that, I still know I could do better. If you haven't heard or learned by now, authors are their own worst critics, and if we don't stop writing and editing, we just keep going until we see perfection. And even then, it still isn't perfect, so the cycle keeps going. It's the world of an author. I hope that you enjoy this read. I love you all! Thank you again for your love and support.

Writing this book came with many challenges. I took a break right after releasing Book 1, and as soon as I started this one, Covid-19 hit, and the world was losing its mind. People were quickly dying, I was furloughed, TK had to take on two jobs to take care of everything, I wasn't able to see my family, and here I was trying to write. It just wasn't working. Call it depression, anxiety, worry, or all of the above and then some; it all played a major part in my delays. From one day to the next, like many others, I just didn't know what I would face. But here I am, two years later, and it is done! Thank you again to everyone who patiently waited for the release. Sometimes in a writer's world, we have to take a break so that we can write about the silence we are in.

www.ingramcontent.com/pod-product-compliance
Lightning Source LLC
Chambersburg PA
CBHW050400030726
47503CB00006B/1942